THE
GIRL ON THE
OUTSIDE

point

THE GIRL ON THE OUTSIDE

Mildred Pitts Walter

SCHOLASTIC INC.

New York Toronto London Auckland Sydney

No part of this publication may be reproduced in whole or in part, or stored in a retrieval system, or transmitted in any form or by any means, electronic, mechanical, photocopying, recording, or otherwise, without written permission of the publisher. For information regarding permission, write to Scholastic Inc., 730 Broadway, New York, NY 10003.

ISBN 0-590-46091-9

12 11 10 9 8 7 6 5 4 3 2 1   2 3 4 5 6 7/9

Printed in the U.S.A.   01

First Scholastic printing, December 1992

Dedicated to the memory of Earl

It is lonesome, yes. For we are the last of the loud.
Nevertheless, live.
Conduct your blooming in the noise and whip of the
whirlwind.

— Gwendolyn Brooks

THE ——— GIRL ON THE OUTSIDE

Chapter 1

"I'll freeze the ice cream, but I'll have to get a bath first," Sophia shouted as she dashed up the stairs. It would be good to get out of those sticky church-going clothes. She felt wilted.

As she turned on the water for her bath, she was flooded with happiness: Arnold Armstrong had asked for an evening visit. This happiness, without worry and anxiety, could not have been imagined when she first knew Arnold was coming home for a brief summer visit. Her excitement had been overshadowed with doubts. Would he even remember her? Or would he still think of her as a special friend? Arnold was the oldest son of the minister at First Methodist, Sophia's church. At nineteen, he was two years older than Sophia, and he had already finished his freshman year at Yale.

Quickly Sophia set the small clock near her bed to alarm at six-thirty, just to remind her not to be late. Then she wrapped her head in a thick towel in final preparation for her bath.

Lying limp in the cool water, Sophia believed this

had to be the hottest day ever in Mossville. She let the water ripple over her as she settled farther into the tub, folding her long legs to accommodate her body. There was a surge of relief. The coolness numbed her.

How pleased she was with herself. She was liked. She flushed, remembering the brief encounter with Arnold in the crush of people after the morning service. He was still in his choir robe, his dark hair damp from the hot, moist air.

"Is it all right if I come by this evening?" he had asked.

She had wanted to shout that it would be super, but she'd only smiled and said quietly, "Yes."

"At seven?"

"At seven." He had looked her in the eyes. She tried to stop the rush of color to her cheeks, but it spread, making her heart feel squeezed in her chest. She turned away abruptly, made her way through the crowd, and waited for the rest of her family near their car.

Now she turned over onto her stomach, bending her legs at the knee, her feet in the air. The movement made small waves that washed over her back. How wonderful — a bath. What if she could stay right there always? But there was ice cream to freeze; and finally there would be school. Yes, summer was over. No more work at Woolworth's; Arnold would be going back to Connecticut; only two more days before school. Could it be possible that on Tuesday, September 4, 1957, things as she knew them might give way to something terribly new?

Why do they have to come to *our* school? The thought of Negroes at Chatman brought resentment. Why did things have to change now? This was Sophia's last year at Chatman High. She had dreamed of being a senior, doing all the fun things: homecoming, senior day, the senior prom, and, at last, graduation. What would the year be like with *them* there?

She now saw the faces of the nine Negroes scheduled to enroll at Chatman as they had appeared on local television and in the newspaper. Three boys and six girls. Only yesterday one of them had shopped at the counter where she worked.

The girl had come in when there were few customers. Sophia watched her hurriedly select bobbie pins, a small comb, and a band of elastic. However, when the girl was ready to purchase the items, Sophia ignored her. The girl waited. A white customer came in. Sophia rushed to help her. Several times Sophia ignored the girl while she waited upon whites who had come in later.

Now Sophia ducked her face under the water and came up smiling. That girl. What patience! Or was she mocking *me*? Suddenly Sophia felt angry. She fought the feeling but it spread. She became confused. Was she angry at the girl or at herself?

"Sophia, are you going to freeze the ice cream?" Burt, her older brother, called up to her.

"Yeah, I'm coming," she said, regretting she had promised. Why had Ida been given two days off, anyway? She should be there to freeze that ice cream.

Slowly Sophia pulled herself up out of the water. The hot air of the room made sweat pour off her. She carefully dried only between her toes, then ran, naked, down the hall to her room.

The sound of voices spiraled up the stairs and Sophia knew her older sister, May, and her husband, Ken, had arrived. She dressed hurriedly in white shorts and white shirt, still tying the shirt in a knot at the waist as she rushed down the stairs.

Everybody had gathered in the backyard where plants, trees, and flowers were cultivated almost to perfection. The trees offered shade, and the flowers gave off their spicy fragrance in the humid air. In spite of the shady loveliness, it was still sticky hot in the backyard. Yet, it was cooler than inside.

Her mother, Molly, was showing May a beautiful yellow rose. The rose, her mother, and May shared a similar beauty, Sophia realized. She both admired and envied their fair creamy skin, light hair, and light eyes . . . the way they looked: fresh, crisp, cool even in that hot weather. She would love to have those qualities, but like her father, Alex Stuart, she was freckled, had red hair, and lively brown eyes. No matter how she tried to be beautiful, she managed always to look like the milkmaid, scrubbed clean.

Burt helped her chip the ice and pile it around the can in the wooden bucket of the freezer. As he concentrated on the task, Sophia marvelled at how well he did things with only one hand. Here he was twenty-five, and he had gone to the Korean War to return with one arm missing. Nevertheless, he typed his own stories for the *Daily Star*.

A calm, collected kind of peace registered on Burt's face as he chipped away at the ice. He was the male image of Molly and May. Sophia liked how his well-shaped nose and mouth and his fair coloring all added up to a look of distinction. If only she had one tenth of their mother's beauty!

As she turned the handle of the freezer, the conversation between Ken, a member of the state legislature, and her father caught her interest. Their discussion of school integration reminded Sophia of the morning service at First Methodist Church.

The pews had been almost full when they arrived. Sophia sensed a somber, hushed atmosphere. Was it the heat — or fear — that had the congregation in its grip? There were not the usual smiles and howdies. Everyone appeared to be repressing joy, withholding. Still, they seemed expectant.

Her father, tall, straight, his red hair and freckles giving him a boyish look, led them to their seats with long strides. Sophia sat next to him with Burt between her and their mother. She loved singing with her father's baritone on one side, and Burt's bass on the other. Her father's singing was as impressive as his speaking. Sophia often wondered what he would have become if he were not Mossville's busiest attorney.

Right then, her father and Ken were talking about legal ways to keep those Negroes out of Chatman. Burt left her alone near the back steps to finish the job of freezing the ice cream, in order to join their conversation. Sophia knew that the heat in their backyard would now intensify.

Ken and her father were allies against Burt. Her brother had the unusual gift of speaking up and saying things that few people in Mossville were apt to say. More than once Sophia had heard her father angrily denounce Burt as a communist. Of course, all her father meant was that Burt liked Negroes a bit too much.

Sophia admired Burt more than anyone she knew, but she, too, often felt that he was "way out."

The slowly turning crank of the freezer brought to mind the monotonous twirling of the big fans overhead at church. The service had progressed from songs to prayer, to collecting the offering, and then to the choral selection before the sermon. Burt sat back, relaxed, soothed by the singing. Their father was on edge, upright in the pew, dissatisfied.

Finally, the Reverend Armstrong rose in his black robes.

Sophia now recalled the minor heat wave she had felt just looking at him.

Without his usual preliminary humor, the minister proceeded in his humble yet impressive way to announce his text reading from Nehemiah, chapter 4, verse 14:

And I looked, and rose up, and said unto the nobles, and to the rulers, and to the rest of the people, be not ye afraid of them: remember the Lord which is great and terrible, and fight for your brethren, your sons, and your daughters, your wives, and your houses. . . .

At the reading of the words her father relaxed, sat back in the pew. Burt's back stiffened, his jaw quivered. What was Burt thinking, Sophia wondered.

Burt's real voice now startled Sophia. "It is the duty of a minister to comfort the people and show them peaceful ways to solutions," he said. "That sermon this morning declared war in Mossville against Negroes in the name of the Lord."

"War was declared when the courts said we *must* let Negroes into our schools," her father said.

"Our schools," Burt shouted. "What do you mean? *Our* schools?"

Has he lost his mind? Sophia asked herself. How could he expect to remain in the discussion if he shouted foolish statements.

Everyone knows the Negroes have their own schools. Chatman High is *ours*.

"They damned well are *our* schools," Ken said, "and we have just passed three major pieces of legislation to tighten our control over them."

"They certainly are *not*," Burt said. "Public schools belong to the public, to the people who pay taxes. Negroes pay taxes in this state. So they have every right to claim Chatman High and any other public school in this state as *theirs*."

"Oh, don't be an ass, Burt," May said. May seldom spoke. When she did it was either to reprimand Burt or to soothe Ken.

Her mother headed for the kitchen. Sophia knew that the pained look on her face was because of Burt. Her mother felt that Burt had lost his way since he came back from the war.

What Burt said was moral and right, Sophia knew; yet she resented his saying it. But in spite of her resentment, she could not help yielding to the strange curiosity, the wondering: What would it be like in the same classroom with Negroes? Heaven forbid such a thought! Her parents would die. Still, the thought brought a rush of excitement. *It might not be so bad.* The impression lasted only for a moment, but that moment was enough to reveal how free Burt must feel when he took the side of Negroes.

The crank was now almost impossible to turn. The ice cream was frozen. The argument went on. Sophia moved away from the back steps and sat near Burt, listening to the discussion.

"We'll soon see what rights Negroes have. The governor hasn't given in yet," her father said. "I'll wager the courts will call a halt to this nonsense before Tuesday."

"I'll wager that the time for people who think like you is over," Burt said. "Negroes will be in Chatman when school opens, or Chatman will not open."

"But they have *their* school. Why can't they leave

us alone?" Sophia shouted. She saw the look of surprised pain on Burt's face. She ran from the yard through the house up the stairs and slammed the door to her room. The noise resounded in the backyard.

Chapter 2

Eva Collins did not wait around while the congregation of Shiloh Baptist Church reluctantly separated to make their ways home through the dusty, unpaved streets. She did not even wait for her little sister, Tanya, nor for her mother who chatted with neighbors on the church grounds.

Eva carefully picked her way through the dry, rutted street to avoid damaging her white sandals. There were too few sycamore and chinaberry trees to blunt the heat. The glare of the broiling afternoon sun hurt her eyes. Sweat poured from her face, around her neck, down her back and bosom. Dampness oozed through to her belt. Eva felt an urgency to get home and undress.

The heat that met her when she opened her front door was not unexpected, but it was disappointing. She often dreamed of entering a room of her own and finding it as cool as a vault. When would she stop dreaming? Dreaming of being waited upon, in her proper turn, at Woolworth's; of sitting in any vacant seat on the bus; of walking through Boyle

Park; of going to Chatman High . . . dreams, dreams. But at last one of those dreams was coming true. She would be going to Chatman.

She went through the house to the back. Roger Collins, her father, sat on the shaded side of the porch, fanning himself to keep cool. Why was he home at this time of day? He always worked overtime, even on Sundays, at the small grocery store owned by the family. Eva was surprised to see him.

"I'm home," she shouted, from inside the screen door.

Her father, more than six feet tall, weighing easily two hundred pounds, was not a church-going man. But he often said he feared the wrath of God, so he loved his neighbors.

"And what did the preacher have to say so long on this hot day?" her father asked.

"Same thing everybody else is talking about — us going to Chatman."

"Eva, you know I'm proud y' one of 'em that's going."

Eva's heart beat faster and for a moment she felt she would cry. She knew that the decision for her to go had not been made lightly. Her mind flashed to the day she and her parents had first heard about the plan to desegregate Chatman High.

Mrs. Floyd, the president of the Mossville branch of the NAACP, had come into their grocery store with two well-dressed men who were from out of town. It was pouring rain.

Eva wished it was raining now to cool this scorching day. She thought of how pleasant Mrs. Floyd had been when she said, "Eva, I'm glad you're here. Maybe you can watch the store while we talk to your mom and dad."

Eva's parents led Mrs. Floyd and the men toward the back into a small room that served as an office. They talked for a long time. Finally, Eva's father called her into the room.

With Mrs. Floyd and those distinguished men about, Eva realized for the first time how shabby the room looked. The unshaded light bulb overhead cast shadows on the dingy white-washed walls. Fly-paper hung from the ceiling with its catch in full view. But when Eva looked at her father, she knew he could hold his own in any company.

Looking at her father fanning himself, she now felt the love for him she had felt that day when he said to those men, "This is Eva, my oldest daughter. I think she might be interested in your plan."

As she remembered this scene, Eva rushed to her room, stripped down to the skin, and took a shower. The water pelting her body, reminded her so of that rainy day.

Mrs. Floyd had introduced the two men. "Eva, these men, Mr. Johnson and Mr. Cook, are lawyers from our NAACP national office. They're here to help get some of us into Chatman High. Think you'd like to go to Chatman?"

Eva's heart beat wildly. "Oh, wow! Me . . . go to Chatman?" she cried.

Mr. Johnson smiled and said, "It's not as simple as that, Eva. We want you to think seriously about this."

"And, of course, we must tell you it will not be like going to your old school, Carver, at all," Mr. Cook said. "In fact, as we have been explaining to your parents, there's possibly some danger involved."

Eva could now see her mother as she looked that day, sitting with her hands folded in her lap, her eyes down. Only the sound of the rain beating on the roof and panes could be heard in the room.

Then her mother said, "Now this danger y'all talkin' 'bout, I don't know if our children can handle it. So I don't know 'bout Eva gittin' involved."

"Audrey," Mrs. Floyd said to her mother, "we know there's *some* risk. But we think there is less risk here. You know our state university was integrated long before the Supreme Court desegregation decision of 1954. I believe if any people in the South are ready for integration, it's the people in Mossville."

"What y' think, Eva?" her father asked.

Suddenly, Eva could see Chatman, the three-story brick building with its tall white columns and great stone lion at its front doors. That lion had always seemed as forbidding to her as the FOR WHITE ONLY signs she saw throughout the town on water fountains, rest rooms, and park benches. The thought of passing through those doors made her shiver with a strange excitement. She didn't know if it was joy or fear. Eva was glad that her mother did not give her time to answer before she said, "Roger, I don't think Eva knows what t' *think* in this matter."

"It's Eva that's gonna be going," her father said. "Eva?"

Eva felt the tension between her parents and sensed the fear in her mother's voice. She looked at the two men and then at Mrs. Floyd. She put her head down. "I don't know." She thought about her boyfriend. Would Cecil be going? "How many of us going?" she asked.

"We're trying to get nine students to enroll," Mrs. Floyd said.

"Hmmm. I . . . I think I'd just as soon stay with all m' friends at Carver." She looked at her father. "I'm not sure it's worth it, if it's dangerous."

"There are a lot of advantages, Eva," Mr. Johnson said. "You'd have much better equipped classrooms, new books, new supplies, and good science labs. . . ."

"You'd even have nice warm rooms heated with steam, not with ol' pot bellied stoves," Mrs. Floyd said. Everybody laughed.

"And credits from Chatman are readily accepted at many colleges and universities if you're planning to go on for a degree," Mr. Cook said.

Again Eva felt that strange excitement. "Maybe . . . but what do you think, Daddy?"

"It's up to you, Eva. Whatever y' decide, I'll back y'."

Eva looked at her mother who still sat upright on the edge of the chair. "Ma, what you think?"

Her mother sighed and slumped slightly. "I don't know. We could find ourselves up a creek 'thout a paddle."

"Who knows, you may be right, Audrey," Mrs. Floyd said. "But if we didn't think the time was ripe, we wouldn't dare ask these children to do it. Your daughter will make history."

"I don't know much," her mother said, "but I do know that a lotta people who make history die in the doing. I don't want Eva dead."

"Now Audrey, *we* don't want Eva dead, but we want the *best* for her. Don't you agree?" her father said.

"Oh, I agree to *that*."

"We don't want any child hurt, even," Mrs. Floyd said. "We now have seven of the nine we hope to get. We'd like you, Eva."

Eva knew she would like to go to the main high school, but she was afraid. Maybe her mother was right. "Daddy, tell me, what you *really* think?"

"I understand y' mama's fears. It won't be easy, no struggle is. But our family together should be able t' do what's gotta be done." He reached over and took her mother's hand.

Eva stood looking from one face to another, not knowing what to do. She did not want to die . . . not to go to Chatman. Not for anything. Then suddenly words that she had heard her father say many times flashed before her: "Dying ain't the worst thing in the world. When y' can't choose what y' wanta do, and where y' wanta go, that, havin' no *choice*, is worse 'n death."

As Eva turned off the shower, the quiet reminded her that on that day the rain had stopped suddenly. The noise of the scratchy ink pen sounded in the room as she and her parents signed permission for her to be registered as one of nine Negroes to be enrolled that fall in Chatman High.

Before she finished dressing, the front door slammed. The rest of her family was home. Eva scrambled. By now she should have started preparing dinner.

"Where's Tanya?" she shouted from the kitchen to her mother who was still in her room undressing.

"She went home with your Aunt Shirley," her mother said.

Finally, her mother came into the kitchen. Most of the food had been cooked before they had gone to church. The chicken pie was reheated. Eva was making Kool-Aid. "Mama, it's just too hot to be eating all this food," she said. "Left up to me, we'd have sandwiches and this Kool-Aid."

"Well, I'm glad it ain't left up to you, missie," her father said. He walked through the back door and began setting the table.

When they were just about finished with dinner, Eva asked, "When is Tanya coming home?" Even though she and Tanya were always at each other, Eva missed her when she was away.

Her mother looked at her, then at Eva's father. "Roger, I think we oughta tell Eva."

"Tell me what?" Eva asked, alarmed.

"Honey, folks sayin' our house might be bombed."

"What?" Eva cried.

"It's nothin' but hearsay," her father said calmly, trying to allay Eva's fear. "But we thought it might be best for Tanya to stay over t' Shirley's. . . ."

"And I want y' t' go t' Shirley's, too," her mother interrupted.

"Are y'all coming, too?"

"I ain't runnin' away from home. And Eva, it's up t' you."

"How come y' always leavin' things up t' Eva?" her mother shouted. "I'm worried t' death 'bout all this. Why can't y' just stand up for once and say Eva ain't going?"

Here they go again, Eva said to herself. She was worried and frightened. Maybe she should not have agreed to go to Chatman.

"Listen, Audrey," her father said. "I understand your worryin' but it ain't no use in y' keep bringin' up her *not* going. She done said again and again she want t' go, and I'm standin' behind 'er."

"I still say I wish it wasn't happenin'," her mother said.

"Mama, maybe it *is* just talk and nothin' to be upset about."

"I'm upset 'cause I know what they do t' us when we try t' git outta our place."

"What's our place, woman?" her father asked.

"Roger, you ain't crazy. You know what I'm talkin' 'bout. I was born and raised right here in Mossville. I've seen with m' own eyes things done t' our people too ugly t' mention in front o' Eva."

"And I was born and raised in Texas, so I ain't no fool. And, I ain't 'bout t' be scared of none but God. I still say, if she wanta go there, I'll back 'er."

Eva listened, feeling that excitement that she

now knew was fear. She knew what life was like for Negroes in Mossville. She rode in the back of the bus, went to a separate school, separate church, lived in a separate neighborhood.

The scene she had been a part of in Woolworth's only yesterday, came full-blown into her mind. She had been in a hurry to catch the bus that ran to South End only once every hour, and the girl behind the counter had kept her waiting on purpose. The same smoldering anger and humiliation she had felt then, crept over her now. *Making me wait while she did nothing until white customers came up. I know what she wanted: me to blow up or walk out without my things. But I wouldn't let her know she could put me through that kind of hell.*

Eva was startled out of her thoughts by her mother's voice. "Eva, I wish . . . well, do you want to go over t' your Aunt Shirley's?"

Eva looked at her mother who had always been joyous, full of life. Now she looked worn with worry, and for the first time Eva noticed gray strands in her mother's hair. Had they been there before all this? She didn't want to do anything to hurt her mother. But she could not let the other eight students down, nor Mrs. Floyd.

Mrs. Floyd had suffered a lot, too, for her and the other students. She was the buffer between them and the lawyers, legislators, and school administrators. And there was her father. She couldn't let him down, either.

"Eva," her mother said. "I'm askin' y' a question."

She looked at her mother. All the love she felt for her rushed forth and Eva thought her heart would break. "I don't know, Mama," she said. "Let me think about it."

She went to her room, feeling weak. If only the heat would let up. It was too hot to think about serious matters. A small gray stuffed mouse on the floor caught her eye. Its floppy ears were almost hidden under a toy vanity that was once her favorite. She picked up the mouse and fingered its ear. How could anyone want to hurt Tanya, a six-year-old? She remembered the day Tanya was born. Then she herself had been nine.

She lay face down on her bed, wishing she had never said she would go to Chatman. She was not a super-smart student — a strong C+ or B— — and her parents were not rich. They didn't even have a telephone at home.

Her mind flashed to that girl again who had made her wait at the counter. *She didn't even know me.* All I wanted was three little things . . . to *buy* them. Could she face a thousand girls like that at Chatman? Suddenly Eva was overwhelmed with fear. She could see their house blown into a thousand pieces. "O God, save me from all this," she prayed.

Maybe she *should* go to her Aunt Shirley's . . . the whole family should go. But how could she tell Mrs. Floyd who had done all of that planning, that she was too scared to go to Chatman. And all the people at the church? They were counting on her.

She remembered the first reading from the Bible that morning:

Ye are the light of the world. A city set on the hill cannot be hid. . . . Let your light so shine . . .

And then her minister, Reverend Redmond, had talked, had talked to them solemnly, as if he wanted to comfort them all. His text was from Isaiah, chapter 11, verse 6:

The wolf also shall dwell with the lamb, and the leopard shall lie down with the kid; and the calf and the young lion and the fatling together; and a little child shall lead them.

Sweat poured off her in the heat of her tiny room. Yet, suddenly she felt bathed, fresh, her mind clear. She rushed through the house calling, "Ma, Ma, I don't wanta go to Aunt Shirley's. Mrs. Floyd wouldn't know how to reach me when we git ready to go to Chatman."

Chapter 3

Shadows lengthened, but Mossville did not cool. Sophia stood at her bedroom window, looking out beyond her backyard. People sat on porches, doors and windows were open wide. The sounds of a Sunday evening spread through the muggy air. Supper dishes clattered and tentative fingers stumbled through "Clair de Lune," while the barking of dogs blended with the hum of the city.

It was not much after five o'clock. In her own backyard Sohpia's father sat in a comfortable chair with a book, her mother was quilt-piecing, and Burt lay in the hammock sleeping. How peaceful her family appeared after that stormy afternoon.

Why had she opposed Burt and made that stupid outburst? Never before had she done such a thing in front of everybody. She remembered the hurt look on Burt's face and again felt the guilt and shame that flooded her when she had fled to her room.

The moment she shouted out had been the moment she realized that her family was falling apart over school integration. She didn't want Negroes in their lives just as she didn't want them in her school.

Her mind was plagued with a nagging fear, with the anxiety she often felt when a storm was brewing. She sat quiet and still in a storm, chilled by lightning that licked the edge of dark clouds like the tongues of snakes, the thunder too far away to be heard.

Sophia now fingered the ruffles on the white organdy curtains at the window and crushed them up around her face, thinking about her Grandma Stuart. If her grandma were alive, she would straighten Burt out.

She sat on the floor beneath the window. In spite of the heat, she was comforted by the coolness of her room. Practically all the furniture in it had once belonged to her grandmother, Sophie Stuart. Sophia had been named for her, pronouncing Sophia with a long *i*, *So-phi-a*.

The room was spacious enough to hold a four-poster bed. And even in summer Sophia insisted on covering that bed with a heavy white candlewick spread that was an heirloom in their family.

"It's nothing but a dust collector," Ida had said when Sophia wanted the bedspread. "It's old and hot and heavy."

"But I promise I'll fold it every night. Please, may I?" Now, sometimes as she kept her promise, Sophia wondered if the beauty the spread gave was worth the trouble.

She liked her room with its pale green walls and white ruffled curtains. The heaviness of an old desk and her bookcase was lessened by touches of color: pale yellow roses, a gold and blue pennant from Chatman High, a delicate hand-painted screen, Burt's gift from Korea, and paintings of her own here and there on the walls.

Now she stretched out on the floor and lay quiet and still, trying to concentrate on the sounds of that early evening, but her mind wandered back to Burt and the nine Negroes. She felt that exciting curiosity she had suppressed earlier, when she wondered how it would be with them in the classroom. Then suddenly she was frightened in a way that she had not been since she was a little girl.

She could dimly perceive an evening, hot like this, when she was about six or seven years old. She had gone with Grandma Stuart to South End, a section of town where only Negroes lived. She rode in the back seat of a big black car while her Grandma drove. The pavement ended abruptly and Sophia found herself in another world, a world of dusty streets and small houses with unpainted sidings. Many of the houses were adorned with pots of ferns hanging on porches.

Twilight was lavender and the people, dark as the twilight, sat on their porches. Soft voices were warmly punctuated with laughter. Sophia remembered the smells of spices, of fish and smoke mixed with dust.

Her grandmother pulled up in front of a house where lots of people sat on the porch. The yard was filled with children playing; smaller ones jumped rope or played tag; large ones played an unknown circle game, singing and clapping their hands. They were having so much fun that Sophia wanted to join them.

"I'll play just a little while," she said to Grandma Stuart. She reached to open the car door.

"Don't you open that door!" The tone startled Sophia and she looked at her grandmother. The look on her grandmother's face frightened Sophia.

"I'll be right here," Sophia said, thinking her grandmother felt she might get lost.

"You will not get out of this car."

"Why, Grandma?"

"Because I say so."

Her grandmother had never spoken to Sophia in that tone of voice before.

Suddenly, Sophia became afraid. She crawled over the seat and sat close beside her grandmother. Her grandmother honked the horn.

Soon a tall, dark woman came out to the car with a huge bundle wrapped in a white sheet.

"Evenin', Mis' Stuart. Your washin' all done, right here."

"Thank you, Letha," her grandmother said, as she put some change into the woman's hand.

Sophia stayed close to her grandmother as they rode home. Her grandmother was unusually quiet. Sophia, still worried and afraid that she had upset her, finally said, "I just wanted to play."

Without looking at her, Grandma Stuart patted Sophia on the knee and said, "They are not our kind."

That was the beginning of many trips with her grandmother into South End. Sophia always rode up front. Sometimes they went in the mornings or early afternoons. The streets were quiet and dusty. Old women, shading themselves with parasols, walked on the narrow shoulder of the road. They seemed to disappear in the dust when Grandma Stuart sped by in her big car.

If it was morning, fires blazed under black iron pots, steam rose from boiling clothes as women punched at them vigorously. Lines and lines of sheets, towels, shirts, and pillowcases dried in the white morning sun.

Afternoons, Grandma Stuart would pull up fast, making the dust fly all the way to Letha's porch where a small round kiln glowing with charcoal was stacked with flatirons. Sometimes Sophia saw Letha over an ironing board as they drove up.

Always Letha's dark face was wet with sweat and sometimes she came to the car with soapy water on her clothes from the washing board. Pale, pinkish hands, crinkled as if pickled by water, opened for the quarters Grandma Stuart placed in them, two for each bundle.

A whiff of fragrance through her window now reminded her of the clean sweet smell of laundry dried in the sun. She remembered the excitement each week of opening the bundles of sheets and pillowcases; and Grandpa's shirts by the dozens, starched and ironed like new. Sophia sighed and stirred on the floor. Twilight was now lavender here, too, and big green and yellow moths fluttered at her window. The air was still hot and muggy, but it was quieter. People were settling for the night.

The ring of the alarm clock startled her. Then she remembered. Arnold was coming at seven! She must hurry. The cool shower pelting her and the thought that Arnold cared made her glow. She smiled as she recalled the day he left for school for the first time. They had wandered to the end of the train station's platform away from the crowd to say good-bye. He held her hands and kissed her cheek. Her heart felt tight in her chest and she didn't know whether she wanted to laugh or cry. Then he was gone.

After laying out her green voile dress, she rushed to do her hair up in a ponytail and tied it with a pale green ribbon. In the warm dampness, her hair curled in small ringlets around her face. After spraying all over with rose water, she felt cooler.

She slipped into her dress and turned to survey herself in the mirror. The capelike collar barely covered the top of her arms. The slim bodice tapered to a full skirt that flattered her small waist. With naturally rosy lips, she needed little makeup. If only there were some magic to make the freckles disappear.

The doorbell rang. She dabbed more rose water behind her ears and dashed down the stairs.

There was something about Arnold that both disturbed and soothed her. His cool self-assurance. The first minutes alone with him could be terrifying. She often felt shy, sure that she knew nothing; she could not find the right words.

Now, as she let him in, he smiled, and she knew that to say, "Hi," was sufficient.

"Hi," he said. "You look fresh and cool . . ."

". . . and *colorful*," she finished the sentence, unable to forget her freckles.

"And beautiful," he said. He held her hands for a moment, as he looked at her and smiled. She blushed and led him through to the back of the house.

"Mother," she called. "Arnold's here."

"Come out where it's cool," her father said.

Her parents liked Arnold so they were pleased that he was taking her out for the evening. After greetings, they parted with her father's words of caution. "Drive carefully now, and remember to be home before too late."

Arnold drove through the quiet streets as the twilight deepened into purple. Warm air scented by a thousand night fragrances bathed Sophia's face as they sped through idle streets shadowed in pale lights. All the stores and shops were closed.

Sophia sat, head back, eyes closed, listening to the frying sound of the tires on the paved road. Even though she was relaxed, she was terribly aware of every inch of her body and of Arnold's presence.

"Where are we going?" she finally asked as she sat up and placed her hand on his.

"A surprise place, but nice. That is, I think so."

Soon neon signs blazed red, green, blue, and white and the trees were now more alive. Stores dimly lighted were open. Small knots of Negroes stood around drinking sodas.

Abruptly the pavement ended. The rutted, dusty road was dark. Outlines of small houses let Sophia know she was in South End. A rush of fear came over her as she rolled up the window to avoid the dust. She sat tense, near the door, her hands stiffly folded in her lap. Where was Arnold going? She looked at him in the glow of the light of the dashboard. He appeared as relaxed as when they had started and he was just as quiet.

Negro couples in their Sunday clothes hugged the narrow shoulder of the road, the men trying to protect the women from flying dust. Soon they came to a frame building shaped like most of the houses, but much larger. All the windows were open and lights shone through the openings, casting squares of yellow upon the ground. Chinaberry trees were black silhouettes in the distance.

Arnold turned off his lights as he slowly drove onto the church ground. The loud singing and music spread through the doors and windows and filled the dark night with a ringing sound. Sophia sensed Arnold's anticipation when he said, "Let's go in."

Suddenly her grandmother's face flashed before her and the fear she felt the day she scrambled over the seat of her grandmother's car returned. She could not move. "No!" she said.

"It's all right, Sophia."

"It's not all right."

"I come often. We're welcome here. I know the minister."

"I will not go in there, Arnold. I can't." She sat trying to fight the terrible fear. "Why did you bring me here?" she asked.

"I like coming here and I thought you would, too. I enjoy the music," he paused. "I . . . I like the people."

She was stunned. She had no idea he even knew about this place, about these people. Why had he assumed that she would want to come here, too? Didn't he know what was happening at Chatman? Suddenly she grew angry.

The loud happy sounds of songs angered her more and she stiffened in the seat. "I don't like being surprised this way, and I don't know why you would do this to me."

Arnold looked at Sophia and a surprised sadness came over his face. "I've never come here with anyone else before. I'm sorry that I didn't ask you if you wanted to come, and now I know that I should have. But I care about you very much, Sophia. I guess my caring made me believe that you would be happy with what made me happy."

She felt tears come into her eyes. She cared about Arnold, too, but he had never given her reason to believe he was in any way interested in Negroes. How could he say he liked these people? "Please, Arnold, let's go someplace else."

They drove back through the dark, dusty streets. Soon they passed a small building, crowded to overflowing. People danced to music that came to So-

29

phia as a throbbing sound, the beat of a giant heart. Her grandmother's words crowded in on her, "They are not our kind."

They rode on in silence, but Sophia was not relaxed. Now she was unpleasantly aware of Arnold's presence. Tense, anxious, she wanted to know what Arnold was thinking and why. Would he want Negroes at Chatman? What had she ever done and said to make him think she wanted to go to such a place? Was he testing to see if she was like Burt?

What if he really did enjoy going to that church? Maybe she should trust him. Surely he would not take her to a place where she could be harmed.

They were now back in a familiar place, nearing Sophia's house. The words to the song that had sounded so alive and cheerful came to Sophia more clearly now than when she had sat under the shadow of the voices.

> *Come and go with me to my Father's house*
> *To my Father's house, to my Father's house.*
> *Come and go with me to my Father's house*
> *There is joy, joy, joy.*

As Arnold pulled alongside the curb in front of her house, Sophia suddenly realized that the singing had come to her as a joyous triumph — a victory for them at *her* expense. The anger she had felt on the church grounds returned. "You want them to come to Chatman, don't you?" she asked, trying to disguise her anger.

"They're coming whether I want them there or not," Arnold said quietly.

She let the anger take over. "You'll be *glad* when they enter on Tuesday, won't you?"

"Sophia, please. I really don't think it matters how I feel."

"I know you'll be glad. You just don't have the guts to say it," she said angrily.

He looked at her and she was reminded again of the hurt she had seen in Burt's face that afternoon. He spoke quietly, "Sophia, our world will not end if nine Negroes enroll at Chatman."

"No. Not *your* world," she exploded. "You don't even go to Chatman, so what do you care?" Tears came and she shook as sobs that she could not control burst forth. "What about me?" she cried.

"Sophia, honey," Arnold whispered as he tried to console her. "I'm sorry. I didn't know you were so upset about this."

She let the tears flow as she rested on his shoulder. When she was calm, she sat up and licked the tears from around her mouth and dried her eyes with the back of her hand. "Oh, Arnold, it's all so silly. But I'm scared."

"I'm sorry I did that foolish thing — not asking you. Forgive me."

"It's all right," she said and smiled.

"I am sorry, but I am not apologizing for telling you the truth, Sophia. Our world will not fall apart when integration comes."

Her anger flared again. "I don't want your apology nor do I ever want to see you again, Arnold

Armstrong." She leaped out of the car and started up the walk with Arnold following.

"Sophia, Sophia, please."

She composed herself and said quietly, but angrily, "Just leave me alone." She stood on her front steps, gathering her strength to watch him drive away.

Chapter 4

As twilight slipped into darkness, the youth meeting at Shiloh Baptist Church ended. Eva stood on the edge of a group listening, waiting for Cecil to put away the hymnals they had used. He would walk her home.

She watched him go about the task thinking how lucky she was that he had chosen her over all the other girls at Carver. Not only was he a brain but, also, he was an all-around athlete, a four-letter man, good at football, baseball, basketball. He also ran track.

Cecil was big and tall, but not bulky. Although at first glance one might think him awkward, he moved with grace, precision, and speed. She would not see him every day because she'd be going to Chatman — that was the one thing that made her sad about her decision.

She remembered the first time he had singled her out to speak to her. She had been waiting her turn to try out for the cheerleaders' team. He walked up to her and said, "How y' doing?"

"I'm scared t' death."

"Don't be. When it's your turn, keep your eyes on me. I'll give you luck."

She almost passed out. The great football star whom every girl on campus would just die for was rooting for her. She was so pleased and excited she forgot to be afraid and made the team. She and Cecil became friends. After the games they went together to the dances, and when he invited her to the junior prom, everybody knew she was his special girlfriend.

Finally, he was through putting away the books. "I guess we can go now. You ready?" he asked, towering over Eva, herself five-feet-six.

"Where are you guys going?" one of their friends asked.

"I'm going home," Eva answered.

"Why ain't you staying for church?" another asked.

"Girl, I gotta make a dress for Tuesday. And I haven't cut the first piece."

"Well, you better hurry 'cause you gotta be looking sharp when you go to Chatman," the girl said.

Eva walked with Cecil close behind along the narrow path that bordered the dusty road. There was a fullness in her chest and she felt shy with him so close. They did not talk even though Eva wanted very much to tell him about her anxiety and fear. Words just wouldn't come.

Neighbors were calling to each other and children

played in the street, rolling worn auto tires and trying hard to avoid the ruts.

Finally Cecil said, "I guess I'll see y' only on Sundays now that you'll be going to tame that mighty lion at Chatman."

"I wish you wouldn't say that. I'm not out to tame anything."

"I wish you wouldn't go."

"You could be going with me, you know."

"I don't wanta go. I'm glad my folks agreed that the decision had to be mine. I don't think it's worth it for me."

"It would help you get into college. You say you *want* to go. . . ."

"I do," he said quickly. "That's why I don't want to waste a year at that place. This is my last year in high school and I want all I can get out of it. I wanta play ball with people who care 'bout *me*; and I wanta look back on this year with good memories. You see, I like Carver."

"Because I'm going to Chatman doesn't mean I don't like Carver," Eva said, feeling defensive.

"Oh, Eva, please. Try to understand, I like you the way you are and I want you to be around" — he stopped and threw up his hands — "but you . . . you don't know what it is I'm trying to say."

Eva looked at him. He was the one person she wanted to be around for, but at the moment she felt that he was trying to make her feel guilty about leaving their school. "What is it that I don't understand?"

"It's not just our school. It's our neighborhood . . . it's *us*. It's the way we think, the way we are."

"I can't see how my going to Chatman will affect us," she cried.

"Eva, baby, you're being difficult."

"Well . . . what. . . ."

"Let me ask you this, you think you can put up with what you're gonna have to go through?"

"Now just what do you mean, go through?"

"I wish I was smart enough to explain what I really mean. Listen, I'll put it this way: At Chatman they don't want what we have to offer. They have absolutely *no* respect for our way. They don't even see us. And you think — if you spend most of your day there five days a week — they'll let you come home happy?"

Eva sighed and walked away toward home.

Cecil followed still talking, "Every morning when you get on campus you'll have to tell yourself — 'now it's being white time.' You'll start talking proper, acting proper, and at lunch time you'll try to swallow that white gravy. . . . After awhile y' won't be acting, you'll *be* white."

Eva laughed. "Cecil, you're crazy."

Cecil laughed, too. "No, seriously, baby, now I wish I *was* going. I don't want you over there all by yourself."

"I'll be fine. We have as much right to be there as they have."

"True. But I'd feel a whole lot better if nine of them were coming over here at the same time you're going over there. That's what I call integration."

"Can't you see, somebody has to break the ice."

"Let it be somebody else, not you," he said.

"Oh, Cec', I've given my word. I don't have much else. I'm no brain, y' know."

He stopped and turned her around to face him. "Hey, don't put y'self down. You have a mind of your own, you're creative . . . different. That's why they chose you. And, you stand by your word, no matter what. And that's what has me afraid, you know."

When they came close to home, the darkness had set in. Her house was without lights. Her mother, with some of the neighbors, sat on the porch trying to beat the heat. Her father was still at the store.

"You've managed to keep me from saying all I'd wanted to say," Eva told Cecil. "Now our time is gone."

He held her hands and drew her to him. "I wanted you to know I worry 'bout you. I know you're gonna go. In a way I admire you, but I'm scared, too."

"Yeah," she said as she put her arms around his waist and leaned her head against his chest. She thought of the conversation at her dining table earlier that day. "You don't know the half of it. I'm scared, too. But I'll be okay . . . I gotta be."

"Will I see you tomorrow?"

"If I get that dress finished. We're invited to a party at Mrs. Floyd's, remember?"

"I'll see you tomorrow, dress finished, or not, okay? That's our last day of summer." He held her close and kissed her. "I'm gonna miss you."

Feeling a rush of joy and sadness, Eva turned and reluctantly went into her house.

Eva laid out her dress pattern atop the black-and-white checkered cotton cloth, wishing she had more time before Tuesday. All the windows and doors were open, yet there was not a breeze to rout the humid air that clung to the small space. The unshaded light blazed its share of heat as it glared down from the ceiling.

Noises from the children still playing in the street seeped in. The notes on the scale of the neighbor's saxophone wailed, jarring on the other night sounds then veering off into sweet song. Eva stood still, listening for a moment. She snapped her fingers, feeling the music, then went on unfolding the dress pattern.

Snatches of conversation from her mother and neighbors on the porch drifted to her, reminding Eva that her mother's fear was real and persistent.

"Yeah," her mother said, "I agreed for Eva to go. But I wish I hadn't."

"I know how y' feel," one of the neighbors said. "It ain't too late t' stop 'er, y' know."

"Girl, you know that husband o' mine. And Eva's just like 'im. Never seen two people mo' stubborn." The women laughed. Her mother went on, "I can only hope she don't go there and come back here so changed we can't live with 'er."

Eva listened and felt a bit angry. Why did people think she'd go through that kind of change.

"My husband wouldn't hear of Eva *not* going. He

truly b'lieves children can learn more in integrated schools. But I wonder if it's worth the worry. Like now I'm worried 'bout 'im at the store by hisself."

The talk reminded Eva of her conversation with Cecil. Just as her father believed integration could bring equality, Cecil believed integration could cause more trouble than it was worth. He was for going to all-Negro schools that were as well-equipped as whites'. His plans were in motion to go to Howard University or Morehouse College when he graduated. She wished there was some way she could change his mind about going to Chatman.

How would she manage, not seeing Cecil every day? She recalled the old saying, "Absence makes the heart grow fonder." The way all the girls made eyes over Cecil, his heart could grow fonder, but for somebody else. What with all the talk about bombs and the thought of losing Cecil, she wondered if she would have signed if she had known then what she knew now?

She finished pinning the skirt and started in on the dress top using solid white cotton. She sighed, thinking somebody has to integrate schools sooner or later. Might as well be me *now*. Would it really make the difference her mother and Cecil thought it would? I'll show them, she vowed to herself. I'll not let going to Chatman swell my head and make me forget who I am.

Finally, all the dress pattern pieces were placed on the cloth. She called, "Ma, come check this before I start cutting, please."

Her mother looked at the layout. "Eva, I don't

think your skirt front is on the straight of that cloth." Her mother quickly measured from the arrow printed on the pattern out to the edge of the material. "No, no, no! Unpin this. Do it right."

"Aw, Mama," Eva cried.

"Don't y' want that skirt t' hang right?"

"It'll hang all right. I don't wanta do all that over."

"Listen, I won't have y' showin' up at Chatman lookin' tacky. Now, y' do it the way I showed y'."

By the time the checkered skirt and the white bodice for the dress were cut out, the children had deserted the street, neighbors were settled for the night. Eva, feeling drained from the heat, started on the tedious work of basting. If only she had more time.

Her mother's friends departed and her mother went to bed. The house creaked in the silence. The cuckoo clock on the wall ticked loudly and Eva wondered when her father would be coming home from the store.

The lone saxophone player started in again. Eva felt the loneliness in his music as she basted the pieces together. The clock struck eleven. Why doesn't he come, she asked herself.

At last she heard her father's footsteps moving fast, almost running up the walk. He burst into the room and Eva was frightened by the look on his face.

"Turn off the light," he said sharply as he closed the door and pulled the blinds.

"What is it, Daddy?" Eva cried.

Her father did not answer, but went on through to the back of the house. Eva followed in the dark. Her father rushed back up front and peeped through the blinds. "There a lotta cars in the streets. All with outta state licenses. I was followed by a carload from Mis'sippi," her father whispered as Eva came back up front.

The clack-up, clack-up of her father loading his shotgun made a weird sound in the darkness. Eva's heart beat wildly with fear.

"Where's y' mama?" her father whispered.

"She's sleep. Should I get her?"

"No. Everything's all right."

They listened in the dark. The long shotgun lay menacingly across her father's knees.

Finally, her father said, "You go on t' bed, now."

"Lemme stay with you, Daddy," she pleaded.

"Do what I tell y', now," her father whispered firmly.

Eva lay in her bed listening to the sounds of the night. The sound of cars in the distance alerted her. She could not breathe freely until she was sure they were not nearing her door. In the stillness a lone mosquito zing-zing-zinged near her ear. She worried about her father, sitting in the darkness alone. Then she thought of Tanya. She was glad Tanya did not have to see their father with a shotgun on his knees. Even though the night was hotter than most she had seen, she lay shivering in the dark.

Chapter 5

Monday dawned. The morning light seeped through the open window of Sophia's bedroom. The curtains were not drawn, but not a bit of air coursed through. Another hot day aborning.

Sophia stirred, tossed about, then woke feeling the ill effects of troubled sleep. Desegregation, Burt's attitude, and now Arnold lay heavily on her mind — like the weight of a sleeping cat. She stretched and sighed, feeling sorry for herself.

She lay looking at the ceiling, her hands folded under her head, elbows near her ears, recalling how she'd been nasty to Arnold. The television had been on in her father's study and she had hoped to escape to her room unnoticed. She was not so lucky. When she reached her room her mother was there with quilt pieces spread over Sophia's bed.

"Back . . . so soon?" her mother asked.

"This heat tires me out, Mother," Sophia said, trying to keep her voice and manner even, normal.

"Where's Arnold?"

"Home, I guess."

"You should have asked him in for some of the ice cream we made."

Sophia said nothing and slumped into a chair with her legs outstretched.

Her mother went on laying the pieces to determine how many more were needed to finish the quilt. She glanced at Sophia. "You all right, dear?"

"I'm fine, Mother," she said drawing herself upright. She smiled. "That's going to be the prettiest of all the quilts you've made. Wish it were mine."

"It's for your dowry. Hope we'll have time to get it finished." She looked at Sophia, winked, and laughed.

Sophia flushed, "Aw, Mother, girls don't have dowries, anymore. You know that."

"Well, for your hope chest, then."

Now Sophia turned onto her side. Hope chest, she thought, and grimaced. Her mind wandered to the things she had been collecting since she was sixteen. They were stored in an ebony cedar-lined chest: two silk sheets, hand-embroidered pillow slips, imported linen luncheon sets and a fine lace tablecloth . . . all carefully stored to be unpacked only after her wedding in her own house. And that Arnold! It could have been a perfect evening. Suddenly she felt angry. Then his face above the white collar of the choir robe appeared in her mind's eye as it had been when he asked, "At seven?"

It was not going to be easy. Why couldn't I have gone into that church? she asked herself. But he had no right. *If only he had told me.* She remembered the warm gentleness and the look in his eyes when he had said, "I've never come here with any-one else before. . . . I care about you. . . ." Her heart leaped and she went cold at the thought of living with her feelings about Arnold. Oh, I was a fool not to trust him, she cried to herself.

Anxious and miserable, she turned out of bed and stood by the window looking into the distance. The stillness of the house blended with the quiet of this Labor Day morning. The pale sky, almost sil-ver, had a smattering of feathery, salmon-pink clouds forecasting the rising sun. Dew sparkled on the grass, refreshing the morning, forestalling the heat of the coming day.

The whole of yesterday crowded in on her and she remembered crying on Arnold's shoulder. Again the words "I care about you . . ." pushed all other thoughts aside. She went back to bed thinking, he'll call and everything will be all right.

She lay trying to clear her mind of all thought but her mind would not obey. If only it wasn't hap-pening, she said to herself as the nine Negroes flashed before her mind's eye.

Finally, there was a blank — darkness. Then she was alone on a long trail that led over a low-lying hill. On each side of the trail small dry bush stub-bornly spread out far and wide all over the valley. The trail led to a place where Sophia knew she was forbidden. But it was a place where she had always wanted to go.

As she walked along, she felt tranquil. She was almost to the hill before she encountered any living thing. Then she passed a woman hidden behind a parasol. Sophia could see only a dingy dress and an apron that covered the woman's ankles, but she knew that the woman was colored and that she was very old. She met two more women just like the first, and not once did the women speak or show themselves. But Sophia was not alarmed as she went on up the hill.

Suddenly, she was on a dusty, rutted street. The heat was almost unbearable. Gleaming white rocks made fences around some houses, while similar rocks were used for walks up to the doors of others. All porches had little kilns glowing with charcoal. There were no people or other living things, but she knew someone was waiting for her. Complete silence made a weird sound in her ears, like the bursting foam of a million soap bubbles.

At last she saw Letha standing in a doorway. Immediately Sophia knew it was Letha who had been waiting. She felt a burst of warm friendship, a happiness such as she had never known. But suddenly Letha disappeared and a crowd of ugly children sprang through the door and captured Sophia. Sophia kicked and screamed. But they quickly overpowered her. Though she twisted and turned she could not get away. They dragged her screaming into the dark hot house.

Darkness and heat bound Sophia as she struggled to come up to the light. Turning and twisting, she finally sprang up. Her heart pounded, her throat was dry, and she was wet with sweat.

The sunlight streamed through her window. A bluejay was chattering at a mockingbird who was mimicking a cat. All of these familiar sounds assured her she was in her room, at home, safe. Still she lay shivering, even though her room was warm from the invasion of the early morning sun.

What an awful dream! Why were so many things happening to upset her! Negroes had never been important in her life. They will not be now, she told herself.

She bounded out of bed and moved about the room, drawing blinds to shut out the morning light. Already the heat drove her in for a cool shower.

In the shower she realized it was a holiday and she had nothing planned. If only she hadn't been so hasty. ". . . never want to see you again." Maybe she should call Arnold and suggest they go horseback riding. *Never*. But if *he* called, maybe.

As she dressed to go down for breakfast, the phone rang. Her heart raced wildly and she hurriedly threw on her robe so she would be ready to answer. She listened at the head of the stairs, hoping. Burt was talking to someone.

Disappointed, she took her time dressing, then sauntered into the kitchen. With Ida away, it was every man for himself. Her father sat hidden behind the paper. His plate with the remnants of toast and bacon rinds had been pushed aside. He grunted a response to her "Good morning."

Half-eaten, too-brown, Swiss cheese toast, and three fourths of a cup of coffee indicated that Burt's breakfast had been interrupted by the phone call. Sophia felt a tinge of anger as she stirred about making toast and hot chocolate. Ida should be here to get breakfast, she thought. Yet any other time, even if Ida was there, Sophia would fuss about the kitchen, anyway.

But this morning she was upset. Only mother would give the help *two days* in a row. Grandma Sophie never would have. Grandma's motto: Train a servant the way you want her to go, and hold a firm rein. That's the way she would run *her* house, Sophia thought, as she rushed to retrieve her burning toast.

She threw out the burnt toast, disgusted with herself. Finally, she asked, "Where's Mother?"

"She's off to bathe in the hot springs today," her father said, turning the pages of his paper.

"Looks like I'll have to work today," Burt said, sliding in in front of his cheese toast and coffee. "Something's cooking out there and I'm afraid it's not kosher."

"The governor's speaking to us tonight," her father said.

"I hope he says something worth listening to," Sophia said.

"The only thing I'm waiting to hear is that a restraining order has been issued on that gutless school board," her father said.

"Could a restraining order keep those Negroes out, Dad?" Sophia asked.

"Judge Pomeroy can keep them out. If he wants to!"

"I doubt if he wants to," Burt said. "He takes his federal judgeship seriously."

"He can be had. We'll see what the governor

says." Their father took the paper and left the kitchen.

Sophia sat at the table wondering if her father was right. Could they really call a halt to the integration? She hoped so.

"What are you up to today, Soph?" Burt asked.

"I don't know. I might go ride my horse. Grit is getting so lazy and spoiled."

"I'm going out toward the stables. If you're ready in time, I'll give you a ride. You need a lift?"

"Yeah, that'll be great."

"Oh," Burt said, "What happened to your chauffeur?"

"What chauffeur?"

"Arnold," he said and smiled.

"Oh, please!" She felt the flush rising and jumped up from the table. She turned away trying to stop it. "Just don't mention him to me today, okay?"

The phone rang. Her heart stood still and her hands went cold. "Get that, Burt," she said.

"You get it. It's for you, I know."

"Please, get it."

She sat trembling hoping it was, then hoping it was not Arnold. What could she say now if he called and asked her to do something after what she had just said. Would she ever learn to keep her mouth shut and her thoughts to herself?

"For you," Burt called.

She sat still.

He came into the kitchen. "For you, Sophia."

"Who is it," she whispered.

"Some girl. Sounds like Marsha."

It *was* Marsha. "Hi, What's up?" Sophia asked, feeling both annoyed and relieved. She was a classmate who suggested that Sophia join her and some more of their classmates at the skating rink around six-thirty. They would skate and talk on this last day of summer vacation.

Sophia agreed. She needed to talk to someone to help her sort out things.

Chapter 6

Eva woke with a start. Her first thought was that she hadn't been asleep at all. She was surprised that the sun was high, the room like an oven. Children were playing in the street, neighbors' pots and pans were clattering. Breakfast was already finished and preparations were underway for the noonday meal. Suddenly Eva remembered last night.

She jumped out of bed and rushed to the front of the house. The doors were closed, blinds still drawn, but her parents were not around. Her heart pounded. Where could they be?

A loud knock on the front door alerted her. Her heart seemed to stand still. Then it beat as though it would come through her breast. She could not answer. Again the loud knock.

"Yes," Eva finally said.

"It's me, Eva." Eva recognized the voice of Mr. Charles, her neighbor. "Your daddy asked me t' keep a eye out. Everything's all right. I'm right here."

"Did they go to the store?"

"They been gone. But everybody on the block's lookin' out for y'."

"Thank you, sir," Eva said through the closed door. She sighed. Why hadn't her mother awakened her, she thought. Left her to sleep all that time. She was annoyed.

It was almost ten o'clock and she hadn't sewn a stitch. She must hurry if she was to finish her dress.

Quickly she put on her clothes and swallowed a glass of fruit juice; it was too hot for food. She put up the sewing machine, wishing she could find a cool spot. But even outside, the sun had already invaded every bit of shade.

After putting up the ironing board to press all the seams, she got busy threading the bobbin. As she watched the thread quickly fill the space, her mind was whirling fast from one thought to another. Tanya, hope she's all right. Maybe Aunt Shirley'll come by t'day. That Cecil! ". . . being white time." She laughed. *White gravy, ugh!* Wonder what it's gonna be like . . . with people I don't know at all?

Suddenly she realized that she had never eaten in the same place with white people in her life. Not in a cafe, at a soda fountain, in a home, at school . . . no place.

She remembered the times she used to go into the drugstore downtown with her Grandma Collins for medicine. How many times she had seen people sitting with tall glasses of ice cream sodas, or frosty Cokes and dishes of sundaes. Her mouth would water.

"Grandma, let's git one of them in a tall glass," she said one day.

"You don't want that old ice cream," her grandmother said. "That stuff's not nearly as good as what we'll make when we git home."

Now Eva threaded the machine, thinking how long it had taken her to learn what her grandmother didn't have the heart to tell her: that she could not have ice cream at that counter simply because she was Negro.

As she pressed open the stitched seams, she was thankful she did not have to wait for irons to heat like some people who still did not have electricity. Takes too long. And it's too hot. Her mind again flashed to her grandmother. What would she think if she were alive? — *her granddaughter going to Chatman and her son sitting behind the door with a great big shotgun.*

Eva could see her grandmother now as she used to look coming down the dusty road from working in people's houses. Eva would rush to meet her and take the day-old newspaper and other packages her grandmother often brought: dresses, not new, but still good, and special goodies — lady fingers, chocolate cherries, and sometimes ham and cheese. Often, while Grandma Collins rested, Eva would read aloud to her the day-old news.

Maybe her grandmother would not be scared. Then she remembered the first time she had seen Grandma Collins break down and cry. Her grandmother was worried because her youngest son, Eva's Uncle Joe, had been put in jail, accused of stealing a diamond ring from a hotel room in which he had never been. Could someone accuse her like that at Chatman? She felt prickly with fear.

Then Eva heard laughter and footsteps. She looked up and her Aunt Shirley and Tanya were at the door. Eva screamed with delight. "Oh, Aunt Shirley, you won't believe it, but I was just thinking 'bout you and Grandma Collins." She hugged Tanya. "And I was hoping you'd come home t'day."

"You act like y'been 'way from each other a year, and it's been no mo'en a day. What y' thinkin' 'bout me and y' grandma?"

"Oh, just hoping you'd come by; and wondering what Grandma would think of my going to Chatman."

"She'd probably be proud and scared. But she was one lady who stood up for what she b'lieved. Took no tea for the fever . . . wore no crepe for the dead. Really had a mind of her own."

"Grandma was a lotta fun, you know. Remember how she used to like to dance? She thought dancing released all the demons and left the body free and relaxed. She knew something about almost everything. Wish she was here t' tell me what t' do now."

Her Aunt Shirley said, "Now, I know she'd tell y' this: 'Don't you go there, now, lettin' 'em sand y' down, and come back here not knowin' whether y' fish or fowl. Y' won't feel good with y' own people, and the other sho' won't feel good with you. You'll have *no* place, then.' That's what she'd tell y', Eva, and I hope you'll remember that."

"My goodness, I'm getting that message from all sides. All I'm doing is going to school. You'd think I'd decided to pass for white." Her voice broke and she was surprised that she was so upset.

Eva looked at Tanya who was standing wide-eyed, listening. "Tanya, go out and play."

"Too hot out there."

"It's hot in here, too. Go on." Then she softened. "And when y' come back we'll make some lemonade." She put her hands on Tanya's shoulders and steered her toward the door. At the door she bent and whispered, "I promise, you can put as much sugar as y' like, okay?"

Tanya grinned and went outside.

"Oh, Aunt Shirley, if things keep up the way they're going, I'll be a nervous wreck before t'morrow."

"You'd better calm down, girl."

"It's too much. You should've seen Daddy last night sitting there with that shotgun. Talk of bombin's. All because of us going to Chatman. What's wrong with people? I'm trying so hard not to be scared."

"It's hard *not* t' be. Remember when y' first went t' Carver? Y' musta been scared then, eh?"

"Yeah, but this is different."

"Whole lot. But everything we do that's a little different help us t' git ready for things that's a lotta difference. Ain't no harm in bein' scared o' somethin' y' don't know 'bout. But just make up y' mind y' gonna go and do the best y' can."

"I . . . just wanta learn. . . ."

"Oh, but y' gonna do some teachin', too. They can learn as much from you as y' can learn from them. Otherwise, what's the point o' this integration?"

Eva picked up the bodice of her dress and sat at the sewing machine. The silence between her and her aunt was somehow sobering. She sighed. "And to think, after I'd first made up my mind, I was so happy and excited."

"It ain't that bad, now. Go on, stitch y' dress and I'll help y' fit it," her aunt said with enthusiasm.

As the dress was being fitted, Eva stood still but her mind was on what she might have to face, not only at school, but at home as well.

Finally, she said, "Aunt Shirley, I'm glad I have you to talk t'. I don't want to upset Mama anymore than she already is. But I don't know what to expect at that school. I'm just wondering if I'll know how to act."

"Honey, you don't have t' *act*. Jist be! Now, me and your grandma, we *had* t' act. I can remember when I used to work in a house that had little children. As soon as the little girls passed twelve, I'd have t' start callin' 'em miss-so-en-so. Now mind y', no matter how old I got, I was still Shirley. Well, when they got 'round ten or so, I'd pick out some kinda sweet name for 'em, peaches, honey-chile, anything, jist so long as I didn't have t' call 'em no miss."

"Aw, Aunt Shirley," Eva laughed.

"Yeah, I did it. But you don't have t' go through

all that. Y' as much student as anyone o' them. Jist
be y'self, that's all!" She stepped back and looked
at Eva to see how the dress fitted. "Eva, honey,
that's a nice dress. You gonna knock 'em dead, girl."

As Eva sewed the markings, she thought, As the
pieces of this pattern have fallen into place, so will
everything else. A smile spread over her face.

Chapter 7

Later that morning, Sophia rode with Burt as he drove through the main street headed toward the outskirts of town. Already the sun was blazing, and the air blowing in the open windows was hot and humid.

Sophia hugged the corner and squinted her eyes trying to shut out the glare of the bright sun. The air shimmered in waves, and the heat made a mirage on the road in the distance that looked like black ice.

She glanced at Burt out of the corner of her eye and as always was amazed at his relaxed composure. His one hand loosely held the steering wheel and his body seemed to be one with the machine. Had he ever taken a girl down to colored town, she wondered as she looked at him. What would he think of Arnold — taking her down there? Her father would probably call a conference with Reverend Armstrong if he knew.

She sighed and slumped in the seat. She wanted to talk to Burt, to ask him so many things. How could he know so much about Negroes? Had he ever been in one's house?

Looking out at the passing cars, she suddenly realized that many of them on the road had out-of-state licenses. She took note: Mississippi, Louisiana, Tennessee, and Mississippi again, and again. "Lots of people from Mississippi in town today," she said.

"Yeah, I'm afraid trouble's brewing. Those visitors probably feel we won't be able to take care of ourselves come tomorrow and the school integration."

"Oh, Burt, can you think of nothing but integration . . . I don't want to hear it."

Burt laughed. "Okay, what *do* you want to hear?"

Sophia flushed. The tone of his voice let her know that he knew there was little else she wanted to know about. She sighed.

Burt looked at her and asked, "What happened with you and Arnold?"

"What'd you mean — what happened?"

"Come now. This is a holiday and he'll be leaving in a few days. Why are you spending a whole morning with a horse?"

"Grit needs some attention." She sat with her eyes on the road, tense and alert to control every muscle.

There was no sound except the hum of the motor and of the tires on the road. She felt more than the heat from the sun. Cold sweat poured down her sides from under her arms and her scalp tingled.

What *had* happened with her and Arnold?

She thought of how she had listened for the ring of the phone, hoping he would call. Why hadn't he? He had insulted *her*. "Have you ever been down in South End?" she asked Burt. The words coming from her lips surprised her.

"Many times. My work carries me all over."

"I don't mean like that. I mean . . . go there like to . . . you know what I mean."

Burt turned to her with a quizzical look on his face. "No, Sophia, I don't know what you mean."

"Well, like to church. To hear them sing."

"Oh, yeah. I've done that."

"Would you take a girl there?"

"Of course, if she were a close friend."

"Have you?"

"Yes."

She slumped in the seat and did not look at Burt. She wanted to tell him what had happened with Arnold, but she was so ashamed now of the way she had acted. But then Arnold had not told her, or even asked if she would like to go.

"Why do you ask that?" Burt asked.

"Oh . . . nothing."

"You know, when May and I were small, Mom and Dad used to take us over to a Negro college to concerts."

Sophia sat up and placed her hands under her thighs on the edge of the seat.

"I remember how dressed up the people were," Burt said. "And it always surprised me how dark some of them were and how some were as white as us. They all were together really having a great time."

"Mom and Dad?"

"Yeah, we went there a lot. But they never came to our school or our church."

"And you weren't scared?"

"No. They welcomed us. But here lately, I've wondered why they did. But I guess they knew already what I had to learn the hard way."

Sophia waited, but he did not go on. She looked at him. He was in the mood that he was often in these days — serious, almost solemn. "What did you learn?" she asked.

"That there are so few real human beings in this world that we can't afford to miss out on knowing one because his or her skin is a different color."

The car entered the dirt road that led to the stables where Grit was boarded. Soon they reached the gate and Sophia got out to walk the distance to the horses. She waved good-bye, thinking of what Burt had said, wishing she understood her brother, knew what he was about.

As she walked up the road, her mind was in a state of confusion. "So few human beings." What did Burt mean? The world is full of human beings, she told herself. Why does he think they are so hard to find? And there are at least ten whites to one colored. One can relate to just so many people at a time. Anyway, she thought, Burt's weird.

The sun blazed down and sweat poured off the side of her face. The cotton shirt she wore clung to her back. Her old twill riding pants absorbed the moisture and she felt the cool dampness around her legs and thighs.

It was nearing ten o'clock when she reached the stables. The place was busy with riders taking advantage of the holiday. The air was close, humid with the sour smell of horses. To Sophia that air was sweet. As she passed between empty stalls she was surprised that so many riders were already on the trail. When she neared Grit's stall she whistled softly.

Grit turned his head toward her and Sophia quickened her step. They met at the edge of the stall and Grit looked her over with his bold questioning eyes, then flung his mane and lifted his arrogant head high.

Sophia laughed. "Oh, Grit," she said, stroking his velvety upper lip, "you sweet devil. We're going out for some fun."

She went out to find Rod, the groom and all-around handy man at the stables. He was nowhere to be seen. Sophia was annoyed. She hadn't planned on grooming Grit and saddling him up in all that heat. But it was late. If she were going to ride she'd have to do it.

As she led Grit out into the sun, his coat gleamed even though she had not curried him yet. Grit moved with lively grace as he turned his head to look around and about. Sophia led him to the cross tie near the tack room and started to get him ready for the saddle.

She was startled when Rod appeared next to

her, as if he had stepped out of thin air.

"Oh!" Sophia said. "Golly, Rod. Shouldn't scare me like that."

"Sorry, Miss," he said. "Thought y' might need some help."

"I do. I'm late starting. Where were you?"

Rod ignored the question and set to work. He had small hands, but his long delicate fingers touched Grit with such assured kindness and firmness that Grit seemed to know exactly what Rod wanted from that touch. Rod was not a tall man. But because he was short from the waist up, his long legs gave an appearance of great height. His arm reach was unusual for one as short as he.

He put the saddle on. As he adjusted the bridle, his dark face, wet with sweat, had a reddish glow. His eyes, a startling, clear light brown, with a blue ring around the pupils, reflected whatever colors were nearby. People were often amazed at the change of color in Rod's eyes. Sometimes they were blue, sometimes green. As he saddled up Grit his eyes were amber reflecting the sheen of Grit's reddish-brown coat that now shone like satin in the sun.

Sophia climbed into the saddle. She looked at Rod as he made final adjustments. It was as though she were seeing him for the first time. *Rod was a Negro.*

The jolt of this recognition passed from her to Grit. He reared up and broke toward the trail. Rod had to move quickly to keep from being sideswiped. Sohia struggled to bring Grit under control as he sidestepped dangerously, light foam at his mouth.

She knew she had to quell her own fear and confusion if she were to control Grit. When it was all over and Grit was in hand, Sophia did not look back but dug in her heels and set off at a gallop.

She rode hard until she came to the path that was wooded on both sides. There she reined in. Grit slowed. Leaves on the trees that had been bright green in early summer were now dark in the heat. It was as though they were dulling themselves before robing in the reds and golds of autumn.

Sohia's mind was awhirl with confusion. How could it be that she had never before been aware that Rod was Negro?

Her thoughts flashed to the day she had rode a horse for the first time. Rod had given her that experience almost nine years ago.

Grit was then young, lively, hard to handle. Sophia had walked straight up to him and looked him over. She touched his firm shank and her hand quivered. She moved her hand up his strong back along the side until she was up to his fine, intelligent head. Looking Grit in the eye, she smiled and touched the white patch on his nose. Grit stood without moving a muscle.

"He likes y'," Rod said in his quiet way.

Sophia put her hand up to her mouth and squealed. She walked away reeling, looking back often. From then on, she behaved like someone in love. She *was* in love — in love with Grit.

Her patience knew no bounds. She worked hard

learning to talk to Grit, to acquaint him with the world of things so that he would not get scared or spooked.

Rod was always there to help her learn grooming, tacking, and to show her how to put Grit through the trail course.

Without Rod's help, she would have given up on learning to ride, for Grit was as stubborn as she was firm and patient. Twice he threw her, but each time Rod insisted she must ride him again. And she had won.

Now, though Grit was a spirited horse with a long, swinging stride, she had him under control. And all of this had been done with the help of Rod, who always called her "Miss."

She rode on the path heading uphill through the silent woods. The whole world seemed to be sleeping in the heat under the noonday sun. A lone butterfly soared briefly, then flitted from flower to flower. Sophia was reminded of the dry, dusty valley in her dream.

Walking with a steady gait, Grit climbed up the trail until they reached a wide bluff that looked down upon a stream far in the distance. Sophia climbed off Grit and, holding the reins, walked to the edge of the bluff. The stream below gleamed like molten silver. Off to one side, she could see an orange bridge spanning the stream to carry freight across. A train slowly puffed its way to the other side. The motion in silence seemed unreal. Then the train's whistle sounded, echoing faintly in the hills.

Now all was still again. Sophia stood, hearing

only Grit's breathing and feeling the heat of his strong body. "How happy you must be, Grit, old boy, not knowing all the troubles of my world," she whispered.

Her eyes filled with tears and she moved around and stood leaning against Grit's flanks, her head on her arms. Grit stood still, as though he were sharing the misery of her confusion. Sophia's sobs sank into the silence of that place.

Chapter 8

By the time Sophia got home, the sun was well across the sky, but its power had not diminished. Sophia now wished she had not promised to meet Marsha and her other classmates at the skating rink. She would just like to fold into herself like the four-o'clocks, little flowers that end their day at four. She was exhausted.

Why was she so tired? she asked herself as she moved up the walk, waving good-bye to a neighbor who had given her a ride from the stable. How many times had she spent the same number of hours with Grit and afterward felt on top of the world? Was it the heat? she wondered.

The quiet stillness of her house with blinds drawn against the glowing sun brought back the loneliness she had felt on the bluff with Grit. It was not just the heat, it was her state of mind.

If only she could understand what was happening inside her. Her thoughts wandered to how she had heeled Grit into a gallop when she should have gone back to see if Rod was all right. Maybe facing Rod would not have been so difficult on returning from her ride if she had stopped then.

On her return, many of the horses were in their stalls and only a few riders were still about. Rod was waiting. She dismounted without looking at him. Even though Rod went through the same procedure — quietly unsaddling Grit, bringing the basket of oats — everything to Sophia seemed different.

Other times she had felt free, talkative, happy, watching Rod's silent ritual that ended with Grit in his stall, being rewarded for a good ride with the oats and a surprise. The surprise was usually an apple or a carrot provided by Rod. But today her self-consciousness in Rod's presence had been almost unbearable. She had tried to talk to Grit, but halfhearted mouthings rattled in her throat. Finally an awesome silence settled around them.

Upon entering the house she found no one home in the cool quietness. The shy humiliation that bordered the fear, which she experienced as Grit ate in the silence, came over her again.

A note near the phone on the small table beneath the stairway said her parents were at May's. Sophia could either join them, or find food on her own. No one had called.

On the way to the kitchen she thought of Arnold. *Why hadn't he phoned?* But standing in the glare of the open refrigerator's light, her mind flashed back to the stables. Suddenly she realized that Rod was usually quiet, seldom speaking to riders unless asked something specific. With the horses he was different — a perfect hand, gentle, yet firm. Rod had not changed.

She stood for a moment, gazing into the glaring whiteness of the refrigerator, not seeing, not remembering what she had wanted. Blinking back the tears, she made her way up to her room.

Without thought of the beautiful candlewick spread, she lay upon the bed, fully clothed, glad no one was there to ask, "How was your ride?"

Again she thought of Arnold not having called and her mind wandered to the conversation with Burt in the car. Mother must have known of Grandma Stuart's warning: "They are not our kind." Then why had she taken Burt and May to hear Negroes sing? Why was I never taken, she wondered. And why was I never told that it happened? Could Burt be lying? Did he dream that when he was a little boy and think it was real? Burt's not crazy — anything but — she thought.

If only somebody would straighten things out. Her world had turned upside down. And it was all because those people were forcing their way into *her* life. She sighed and pulled off her boots.

Four forty-five by the clock; she had a few moments to rest. If no one came to give her a ride, she would walk to the skating rink. It was only ten minutes away. She sank into the sofa bed, her body heavy with fatigue.

She dozed. She was on Grit, thundering wildly through a wooded path, escaping from Rod. Suddenly she sprang up rubbing sleep from her eyes.

It was now a quarter to six. To meet Marsha on time, she must hurry.

In the shower she decided to skate in her very special outfit — the white one trimmed with green. Arnold might be there.

The house was still quiet and lonely as she ate graham crackers and drank some milk. Suddenly she realized she was really hungry. She hadn't eaten since breakfast, but there was now too little time. Enjoying the cold air from the refrigerator, she scooped homemade ice cream out of the container with a soup spoon. She had to hurry.

The noise at the skating rink was almost bedlam when Sophia arrived. The place was crowded even in the recessed carpeted area where she walked, scanning the circle of skaters looking for Marsha. Marsha was not among them. Sophia decided to change; then she could skate, while she looked.

The girls' locker room was also crowded and noisy. As soon as Sophia entered, Marsha rushed to her screaming in delight, "Sophia, we thought you'd never get here."

Sophia was immediately surrounded by Kim, Stephanie, and Lila. Meredith stood back. Her large marine-blue eyes shadowed by long black lashes looked beyond Sophia and the others. Sophia held up her hand to the crowd and said, "Hey, hold off, let me get dressed."

"Yeah, and hurry," Kim said. "There're loads of guys out there."

Sophia, pretending not to notice Meredith's aloofness, said, "How're things, Meredith?"

A half-smile spread over Meredith's naturally light brick-red lips. Aware of her freckles and her open enthusiasm, Sophia flushed, wishing she could achieve such a cool effect.

As Sophia dressed and adjusted her ruffled collar in the full-length mirror, she knew she had on the most attractive outfit by far. The green trimming did wonders for her red hair and bright brown eyes. The long fitted sleeves and the special collar played down her full short skirt and tight fitting panties beneath it.

How pleased she was when Meredith fingered the ruffle and said, "That's a nice outfit. Where'd you buy it?"

"Our dressmaker designed it."

"Oh, I just knew it had to be made special. It's lovely."

Sophia flushed and put on her white roller skates, happy that she had decided on green tassles.

"Hurry up, Sophia, we'll miss the partner's whirl," Kim said.

"Oh, Kim, there're other things besides boys, you know," Sophia said.

"What, for instance?" Stephanie asked.

"Our school's invasion, for instance," Marsha said.

"That!" Lila said. "It's out of the question . . . beyond our control."

"No such thing — beyond our control. We'll be

on campus and in the classroom with them. It's our *problem*," Sophia said.

"Oh, for crying out loud, let's just skate and forget it." Kim was losing patience.

"*Niggers* are no problem," Meredith said in her aloof, cool way.

Sophia looked up surprised that one in the group had the nerve to say that word. But the giggles of the others were contagious and she laughed, too, not knowing why. Then there was a sudden silence. Meredith had their attention.

"I just *see* no niggers, *hear* no niggers, *speak* to no niggers."

"What a great idea," Sophia said enthusiastically. "We can just ignore them."

"As if they were really *not* there," Marsha said.

"Then the year will be *ours* as all the years have been for seniors," Lila said.

"Let's make a vow," Sophia said. "Join hands, criss-cross fashion, close our eyes, and solemnly swear that we will see no . . . can we say darkies?"

"I prefer *niggers*," Meredith said.

Sophia sighed, exasperated.

"Let's vote on it," Marsha said quickly.

Sophia won.

"I think I have a better idea still," Sophia said. "Let's not say anything so that only those we tell, *and they must be seniors*, will know what we are about."

"How can we do that?" Kim asked.

"Easy. Use our hands only. Over the eyes, *see*

no darkies; over the ears, *hear* no darkies; and over the mouth, *speak* to no darkies, okay?"

"Great!" Marsha said. "Then the powers that be, meaning teachers, won't know what we're about, either."

"Oh, girls," Sophia said, hugging them all in a circle, "we've done it."

"Now, can we go skate?" Kim asked.

"What if somebody breaks the vow?" Meredith wanted to know.

"Oh, we wouldn't," Marsha said as if surprised at the thought.

"Somebody might. And if they do?" Meredith insisted.

"Then we'll brand them traitors," Sophia said.

"Just traitors? Must be stronger than that," Meredith said.

"Oh, *let's go*," Kim pleaded.

"Who's out there you can't wait to see, Kim?" Stephanie asked.

"Everybody! And what's worse than a traitor, anyway, Meredith?"

Meredith's eyes searched each face in the circle with a look of suspicion. Then she said in a voice that was a hissing whisper, "We'll brand them *nigger lovers!*"

Burt and Arnold! What would they think of this vow? Sophia felt a tremor over her body, but she joined in the giggles with the rest of the girls.

After they moved out of the locker room, as soon as Sophia got a chance, she cornered Marsha. "That Meredith. What nerve, using *that* word."

"She just doesn't want them at Chatman," Marsha said.

"You think I want them there? Do you?"

"Of course not. But you know a lot of people use that word, Sophia."

"Not my friends. . . ." Sophia placed her hands on Marsha's shoulders and held on, looking Marsha in the eyes. "Fortunately, *not my friends*." She grinned and then skated off through the crowd, her eyes and mind alert for Arnold.

Over the din, the loudspeaker announced a skating round for girls only. Sophia rolled gracefully along, telling herself that she must forget Arnold and have a good time. Whenever she skated by one of the pact members she gave part of the signal: hands over eyes, then over ears, then mouth. They would crack up with giggles.

Then it was time for partners to skate together. She watched Kim, Marsha, and the others scramble for a partner. Suddenly it all seemed so childish, with everybody appearing so young. It really was not much fun anymore. She wanted to get home. In spite of the pact, there were still questions that had to be answered before she could really cope with the coming tomorrow.

Chapter 9

Shadows lengthened. Mockingbirds sang. Blue jays screeched at the hummingbirds darting swiftly to suck nectar from honeysuckle vines. Eva sat on the back porch, putting the last stitches in the hem of her dress. Smells of fresh rolls rising in pans and chicken sizzling made her hunger almost unbearable. How glad she was her Aunt Shirley had not listened to her pleas not to cook because of the heat. Would she be able to wait until her parents came before getting at the food?

She listened to the birds' songs. How nice it was to have her dress finished on time and to hold to her heart the pleasure of knowing she would be seeing Cecil later. The thought forced a silent spring of joy. She smiled. If her good fortune lasted, she could get a bath and even rest a few minutes before supper.

Humming a tune that made her aunt smile, Eva passed through the kitchen on the way to her room. Eva stopped, sniffed the air, closed her eyes, and pretended she was going to faint. "Oh, I'm starved."

"Here, take a wing. That'll hold y'," her aunt said, giving Eva a piece of fried chicken.

On entering her room, Eva's hopes for a peaceful rest were shattered. "Tanya," she shouted, "how could you junk up this room like this? Clean it up, right now."

"I'm busy," Tanya said, without looking up. She was dressed in one of Eva's skirts and a pair of their mother's high-heeled shoes.

"You pick up all this stuff and get out of here!"

"It's as much my room as yours."

The front door slammed and their father's voice boomed through the house. "I know my sister's here. I can smell it." His laughter mixed with their mother's made Eva rush to the front of the house.

"You'll clean up now, I bet. Mama's home," she shouted to Tanya.

"Here, Eva," her mother said, unloading packages in Eva's arms.

"What's all this?" Eva asked.

"Unwrap 'em and see." Her mother sat and kicked off her shoes.

"What's for me, Mama?" Tanya asked.

"My open arms. Come in 'em." Her mother hugged Tanya close. "I missed my baby."

Eva unwrapped the packages. "Oh, Mama," she cried. "Aunt Shirley! Come see . . . saddle oxfords, black and white ones."

"Just what y' need with that dress. She'll knock 'em dead in that outfit, t'morrow," her aunt said and winked her eye at Eva's mother.

"Why you lookin' so sad, Tanya?" their daddy asked.

"I don't get jealous when Mama buys you things," Eva said.

"Aw, shut up," Tanya said.

"Rejoice all of y'," Aunt Shirley said. "I done cooked fried chicken, green beans, made rolls, potato salad, and for my brother, a lemon pie."

"I'll say rejoice *plus* let's eat," Eva said, forgetting that she wanted to rest.

Trying to keep cool, they all gathered on the back porch for supper.

"Ain't many sister-'n-laws like my sister-'n-law," Eva's mother said as she went for seconds.

"Yeah, it's a good thing Aunt Shirley came by, or I'd never have finished my dress. Mama, how come you left me sleeping this morning?"

" 'Cause I told 'er to. After last night, y' needed that sleep," her father said.

"Y' shoulda seen y' brother this mornin', Shirley. Sittin' b'hind the door, nodding with the gun in his lap. I woke up and he hadn't been in bed. When I saw that gun, scared me nearly t' death."

"Which way was the gun pointin', Audrey?"

"Toward the door I was comin' through. I didn't know what t' do. I didn't want 'im shootin' me. So I tipped around in back of 'im and said very sweetly, 'Roger, Roger, wake up.' "

"Y' was ready, eh, Bro?" Shirley said as they all laughed.

"I guess I musta looked a bit funny sittin' there

in broad daylight. But I'm about protectin' my family," her father said.

"And Mama slept through it all. It wasn't funny last night," Eva said.

"Daddy, how come y' had the gun?" Tanya asked.

"That's grown folks talk," Eva said. "You come with me and clean up that room."

"I don't have t'," Tanya said.

"Oh, Eva, I forgot, Mis' Floyd wants you guys that's goin' t' Chatman at her house 'fore the party. 'Round six-thirty, she said."

"That leaves me little time to get way over there. Come on, Tanya."

"No."

"Mama, tell her, please."

"Go on, help your sister, baby."

"Why do you take everything out and put nothing back?" Eva asked as she busied herself about the room. "I can't stand all this clutter, you know that."

"I guess y' want me t' stay with Aunt Shirley, eh?"

Eva felt a pang of guilt, but she was still angry. "I want you to stop being so messy." She looked at Tanya standing with the big, long skirt pinned around her small body. She thought of why Tanya had gone to their aunt's in the first place. She softened. "I told you I was glad t' see you home, didn't I?"

Tanya looked up at Eva and remained silent.

"Didn't I?" Eva asked, feeling even more guilty.

"Yeah, but y' didn't mean it." Tanya lowered her head.

Eva took Tanya by the shoulders and drew her close. "I meant it, Tanya."

"Why'd Daddy have the gun?" Tanya asked, still in Eva's embrace.

Eva stiffened. "He was protecting us."

"How come?"

Eva moved away from Tanya and busied herself picking up a cardboard puzzle. "Oh, because. . . . " She didn't want to talk about it. Tanya didn't need to be as upset and frightened as the rest of the family.

"How come y' wanta go t' that school?" Tanya asked.

"Oh, Tanya . . . it's a good school."

"Better 'n mine?"

"It's bigger than yours. And when you're bigger, you might wanta go there. I wanta go there so *you* can go there, too, okay? Now, let's clean up so I can get ready and get out of here."

In an uncluttered room, Eva laid out what she would wear and dashed into the shower. She hated to rush, but she was glad to have shared supper with her parents. She recalled the laughter on the back porch and smiled, pleased that her mother had made them all laugh. Maybe things would be all right as her aunt said they would be. How could they *not* be with neighbors like Mr. Charles and a family like hers. She thought of Cecil and sang in the shower.

She presented herself on the back porch in a pale

yellow organdy dress with yellow and white daisies pinned at her slender waist above the wide flowing skirt. When her family looked her over from her pearl earrings to her white sandals, they were pleased.

"Honey, that's what y' oughta be wearin' t'morrow," her aunt said. "Y' look like Mis' Lena Horne, herself."

"This is a party dress, Aunt Shirley," Eva said, feeling a bit self-conscious.

She looked at her father and remembered when she was a little girl how she would ask, "You like my dress, Daddy?"

"It's okay."

"You think it's pretty?"

"What's pretty?"

She had learned to study his face to see if he approved or disapproved of what his womenfolk wore.

Now he smiled. He was pleased and Eva felt good inside.

"I'll drop you off and pick you up later," her father said. "I want t' git back and listen to the governor. Y' jist might not be goin' t' Chatman t'morrow, y' know."

"Now, don't go puttin' the cart 'fore the horse, Roger," her aunt said. "Don't read the man's mind 'fore he reads his speech. Let's wait and see. Anyhow, now we done made that dress, *nobody* better not say she can't go. I'll take 'er up there m'self after all that work."

Eva laughed and said, "If anybody can do that

and get away with it, it's you, Aunt Shirley."

"Eva, you go on and have a good time. If you as nice there as y' look, Mama'll be mighty proud."

Eva and her father left, laughing.

Still waving good-bye to her daddy, Eva hurried up Mrs. Floyd's walk to join Lisa and Roberta who were also arriving.

"We're late," Roberta said. They all called Roberta, Bobbie.

"If everybody else is here they'll blame us for holding up the party," Eva said.

"Now they know we wouldn't do that on purpose," Lisa said. "Not me, anyway, the way I like to party."

Everybody else was there. Harold was off to himself looking at *Crisis* magazine. Ronald and Arthur were together talking about football practice at Carver, and the other girls, Janice, Mary, and Lillian, were in the kitchen helping Mrs. Floyd put together the sandwiches and punch for the evening.

"We can finish this later, girls," Mrs. Floyd said. "Let's go downstairs in the rec' room and get the meeting over. Won't take long."

"You mean there'll be no great decisions, today, Mrs. Floyd?" Eva asked.

"I'll let you guys decide that. *I* don't have anything new. Not yet, anyway."

They all gathered downstairs, laughing and talking — in a great mood.

"This time tomorrow, we'll know what it's all about," Harold said.

"If the governor doesn't blow the whistle and stop the show," Arthur said.

"He has to abide by the federal law even if he is governor," Eva said.

"There're ways, eh, Mis' Floyd?" Arthur said.

"We hope he doesn't find any," Mrs. Floyd replied. "But you know the governor. We don't know what he's going to do. As for now, I have the school superintendent's word you'll be going tomorrow."

Eva felt a surge of joy, and for the moment she forgot she had ever been afraid. She looked around the room. She caught Bobbie's eye, and responded to Bobbie's smile. How happy she was to have been chosen with this group.

Of the six girls only Lisa, a freshman, was younger than Eva. All the other girls were juniors, a year older than she. Ronald and Arthur were juniors, too. Harold was the only senior as Eva was the only sophomore.

Mrs. Floyd sat in the middle of the group and talked in a quiet friendly voice. "I hate to keep reminding you, but it is important for you to know that . . ."

" . . . this is no picnic." Eva finished Mrs. Floyd's sentence.

"Eva, you got that spiel down pat," Bobbie said, and everybody laughed.

"I want *all* of you to get it down pat," Mrs. Floyd said. "You'll be out there on your own and you must use the 'buddy system' as we've planned. Try never to be alone when you are outside of the classroom."

"Nine out of two thousand," Ronald said. "We'll need to stick together."

"Indeed!" Mrs. Floyd glanced at them with a look more solemn than Eva remembered. "There are a few students who want you to come to Chatman. There are a few who don't want you there and will do all in their power to make it miserable for you."

Eva looked at Bobbie, happy that they were buddies. They would support each other, be together on the grounds and in the halls.

"Just so they don't hit me," Lillian said. Lillian was tall, an outstanding basketball player who had had to think twice about going, for none of them would be allowed to participate in any sports, or other extra-school activities their first year there.

"I don't want anybody *spitting* on me," Eva said. "I think I could take anything but that."

Everybody started talking at once: "Don't call me names. . . ." "Don't step on my heels. . . ." "Don't kick me. . . ."

"Now, now," Mrs. Floyd said. "There's likely to be some or all of that. But I want you to promise you'll control your tempers to the point you'll not act the way they do."

"That's gonna be hard, Mis' Floyd," Lillian said.

Eva glanced at the faces, trying to imagine how she could let somebody hit her and not hit back. "Why do we have to take that?" she asked.

"Get it into your head, most of the students really have not decided whether they want you there, or not. They are neither for, nor against, your being there. So you must act in a way that, if they have to take sides, they'll choose *our* side. See now? You must understand what you're being asked to do."

There was silence. Eva thought of the Scripture — "Ye are the light of the world. A city that is set on an hill . . ." — and once more she felt a little afraid.

Mrs. Floyd broke the silence. "Now, you'll all meet your buddies in the morning and you'll go together as we planned. If that plan changes, I'll call each of you and let you know. Any questions?"

The doorbell rang.

"The others are arriving. Let's have our party now," Mrs. Floyd said, and she started up the stairs.

Eva quickly joined her. "Mrs. Floyd, I don't have a telephone."

"I always forget. I'll come and let you know, as I always do."

People were arriving fast. Eva stayed upstairs and Bobbie joined her to help Mrs. Floyd finish the refreshments.

"Cecil coming?" Bobbie asked.

"Yeah."

"I passed Carver today," Bobbie said. "Saw him out there in all that heat for football practice. He just might not show tonight."

"He will . . . he'd better!"

Mrs. Floyd took a tray of sandwiches downstairs. As soon as she was out of hearing range, the girls huddled together.

"Eva, you scared?"

"Yeah, somewhat," Eva answered. "If only I knew what to expect."

"She just told us. Expect to be dogged. Girl, I don't know if I can hold my temper."

"We'll have to. You heard what she said. We're the example."

"Guinea pigs," Bobbie said, taking a tuna sandwich from the tray. "I'd make a better other kind of pig." She laughed.

"It's gonna be . . ."

Eva quickly changed the subject as Mrs. Floyd came into the kitchen. "What you gonna wear tomorrow?"

"Mama surprised me with a dress, and I don't like that kind of surprise. But it's a nice dress."

"You couldn't have tried it on in the store, anyway," Eva said.

"I know! Doesn't that just burn you?"

"Well, girls, one of these days, and it won't be long, you'll go into the store and try on shoes and dresses before you pay for them," Mrs. Floyd assured them.

"I like what you have on," Eva said to Bobbie as she tucked in the facing at the back of Bobbie's dress. The vanilla colored cotton dress had a scooped, round neckline and tiny buttons down the front to the waist.

Eva thought Bobbie, with her glowing brown skin and long black hair, was the prettiest of the six girls. When Bobbie smiled, her round face dimpled and her laughter rang out of complete abandonment.

Now as Eva smoothed the facing, she knew Bobbie was her best friend.

"Eva, you bring the punch bowl. Bobbie, carry this tray and I'll bring the rest. I think everybody's about here now," Mrs. Floyd said, leading the way downstairs.

The crowd had increased. Most of the seniors from Carver were there. Eva moved about, wondering what had happend to Cecil. Surely he would not stand her up.

Mrs. Floyd arranged the food on the table and announced that she was going up to prepare her husband's supper and watch the news. "All I want you to do, now, is have a good time."

The mood of the crowd had changed from what it had been when the nine students had first arrived. Now there was food and good music, but everybody sat around alone, or in little groups, subdued.

Eva wandered over to Harold who again was engrossed in *Crisis* magazine. "Don't you ever get tired of reading?" she asked and smiled.

"No," he said, without looking up.

"Aw, come on, Harold. Put that magazine down. This is a party."

"All the people in this room, why you have to pick on me?"

"Cause you're so serious. You're serious as a heart attack, man."

He laughed and closed the magazine.

She laughed, too, then said quietly, "Are you worried?"

"In a way. But if they give us only half a chance, I think we'll make it."

Just then Eva heard fast footsteps on the stairs. Cecil burst into the room.

"Where's the party?" he shouted. "Hey, you guys haven't gone to Chatman *yet*. Come on, let's let the good times roll. Let's party." He made his way toward Eva.

Eva waited with a bright smile on her face. The room suddenly took on a different glow. Her heart raced under her thin dress as Cecil took her hand and led her to the center of the floor. They danced.

Before long everybody was dancing. The sandwich trays emptied and the punch vanished. Noise swelled and over the shout, "It's show time," Eva got herself together to do her number.

Chapter 10

Street lights were already on when Sophia emerged from the skating rink. It was just minutes before eight, that hour when those who were spending the evening out were gone and those staying in were settled to some activity. The streets were quiet.

The area was familiar and Sophia had walked home many times before, enjoying the night fragrances and sounds. But tonight, even though houses were lighted, windows and doors were open, and people could be seen on porches and inside, Sophia felt uneasy.

She hurried down the street not seeing the distant stars, not hearing the night birds and crickets, not smelling the honeysuckle vines. Alert to some unseen danger, her whole body was intent on getting home.

As she entered her street she suddenly became aware of her fear and was annoyed. Why am I afraid, she asked herself. Why this feeling of shame, guilt, and anger?

Did it have to do with the curiosity she felt about Negroes? That Burt! How could I have ever thought it might not be so bad knowing them? I must never stray that far again. Her mind flashed to her disbelief of Burt's assertion that their parents had gone down to colored town with him and May.

She would ask her mother about that this very evening, she told herself. But did she really want to get to know Negroes? No! She wanted no part of them. Hadn't she just formed a pact to ignore them? She thought of the brilliant idea she had helped formulate and felt a rush of pride. *They are not our kind.* Ignore them and everything will be all right. *But she would ask her parents about what Burt had told her.*

Lights were on in her house and she felt a surge of relief that she would not be alone. She hoped that May had sent her some supper. I'm starved, she told herself.

Her mother and dad were in the small study off the hall. Sophia went in, kissed her father on the forehead and sat near her mother. "Haven't seen you all day, Mother," she said.

"I got an early start. Good thing, too, the spring was crowded."

Sophia looked at her mother whose face was glowing. "You look great."

"What was your day like?"

"Good. Burt drove me out to the stables."

"Did you ride with Arnold?"

Sophia's heartbeat quickened. "No. Did he call?"

"Not since we've been home. Where were you after riding?"

"Went skating, but that was just so, so. Too crowded." How could she ever get the conversation back to Burt now? She had missed her chance when she did not follow through on his taking her to the stable, she thought. She had to know if what he had told her was true, yet she could not bring herself to ask. "Did May send me some supper?"

"She sent you some angelfood cake," her mother said.

"You feel like an angel?" her father asked.

"No. I'm hungry as the devil," she said without laughter.

"Your brother should be home any minute, starving, too. Deserve that cake by making enough supper for him," her mother said.

"Why me? *You* gave Ida two days off and because of your generosity, I've had nothing to eat all day," Sophia's voice betrayed annoyance.

"Is that Ida's fault? You'd better learn to get on without Ida," her mother said ignoring Sophia's tone.

"I guess I'd better. Like the rest of them, she'll be calling the shots and you'll just cave in."

"Wait a minute, young lady. You don't talk to your mother like that," her father said firmly.

Sophia slumped in the chair, not understanding why she felt so angry. Why this sudden animosity toward Ida who had been in the house as a servant as long as Sophia could remember? Always it had been Ida to whom she had gone when everyone else refused to understand her. Never before had there been any doubt that Ida was the one person upon whom she could depend.

The quiet in the room disturbed her, and suddenly guilt replaced her anger. Was it her mood that had ruined the harmony that existed in the room earlier? What was happening to her? She still wanted to know if her parents had ever mixed with colored people the way Burt said they had. But how could she ask that now? Why had what she said about Ida brought such a response from her father? He never cut Burt off. No. There were long clarifying discussions with him!

Suddenly her mind went back to Rod and she felt a terrible pang of guilt. She longed to place her head in her mother's lap and beg forgiveness for what she had said about Ida. She wanted assurance that everything was all right. Then she could feel free to ask them if what Burt said was true. She sighed and asked, "Where is Burt?"

"He's out trying to get a scoop on the governor's speech," her father said. "But that's a well-kept secret. No one will know until we all know in about an hour."

Sophia sat up, determined it was now or never. "Mom. . . ."

"Yes."

"Oh, never mind. . . ."

"What is it, dear?" her mother asked with so much warmth that Sophia was encouraged.

"Did you ever go down to colored churches?"

"No . . . I don't remember."

Sophia flushed. Her heart beat faster and she tried to control this unexpected happiness that came out of knowing her parents had not done such a thing. "You and Dad never took Burt and May to hear colored people sing?"

"Oh, that. Not at a church, dear. But that's so long ago. Honey," she turned to her husband, "what was that colored school?"

"That Baptist college? My, my, that's been years ago."

"Did you go there?"

"Yes. We used to. I remember. Oh, and could they sing," her mother said.

"And you sat with them?"

"Well, we had special seats," her father said.

"Why . . . why did you want to go there?" Sophia asked in dismay.

"I was on their Board then," her father said matter-of-factly. "I'd forgotten that, those were pleasant times . . . no pushing then for the mingling of the races."

"They had very special concerts that were excellent. Especially at Easter," her mother recalled with enthusiasm.

Sophia felt a sudden letdown. Why hadn't they mentioned this before? Didn't they know that Grandma Stuart had forbidden her to even think of going among those people? "Why didn't you tell me you had done that?" Sophia asked. The tone was sharp.

Her father, who had his hand on the knob to turn

on the television, straightened up and looked at Sophia.

"Why, Sophia!" her mother said. "What's with you this evening?"

"You never asked. And how did you find out?" her father wanted to know.

"Burt told me."

From the hall, Burt's voice came in loud and clear. "And what did Burt tell you?"

"It's no secret and no big thing," their father said.

"I don't know what has gotten into Sophia these last few days," their mother said.

Suddenly there was a loud rumbling noise.

"What's that?" their father asked, alarmed.

"Sounds like war," Burt said.

"Oh, Burt, you having one of your nightmares?" Sophia asked, wanting to be mean.

The noise increased steadily. Sophia ran with Burt to the nearby street.

It was not one of Burt's nightmares. It was real. The traffic was halted; people stood outside their cars; children bicycled and roller-skated to the scene. A long convoy of brown, canvas-topped trucks loaded with soldiers in battle dress helmets, boots, and rifles with bayonets fixed was rolling down the street.

Sophia screamed over the roar. "What is this?"

Burt, too, was amazed, but realizing that she was frightened, he said, "Don't worry. The governor must have called up the Guard. They certainly aren't here to harm anyone."

The crowd stood as if frozen in confusion. They

did not cheer the soldiers as a liberating force, because they did not know who the soldiers would help. And the soldiers did not wave and greet the crowd. With the grinding and groaning of the motors, Sophia felt that machines were in control.

The long convoy rolled away. Sophia stood with Burt, not knowing what to think. She did not like the angry feeling rising in her. Was the guard there to force her to swallow nine Negroes at the point of a bayonet?

Finally she said, "I'll bet all this is to get those Negroes into Chatman."

"Surely, Sophia, it doesn't take the army to get nine kids into school."

"You sound as if it's just a simple matter, an everyday affair." She tried to control the rising anger she felt at Burt.

"I should think it's not a matter for the U.S. Army."

Burt's calm reasonableness angered her more. "Forget it, Burt. By now, the whole world knows what you think." She quickened her step, and left Burt behind.

The sound of the television in the study scared her more. The governor already was speaking:

. . . I have asked Judge Pomeroy to issue restraining orders to delay integration at Chatman High School. I am also asking Negro parents to keep their children home. . . . Outsiders bent on preserving the white way of life, are pouring into our city. . . . Blood will flow in the streets if Negroes try to integrate. . . . Therefore, I have called in the National Guard to protect our citizens and property. . . ."

Sophia listened and all the anger and frustration she had felt in the past days combined with the terrible fear that the governor's words provoked. She rushed to her father, "What's happening to us?" The tears gushed forth and she clung to him sobbing. "There're soldiers out there, in *our* streets . . . everybody's against *us*."

Chapter 11

The party was over. Those who were not going to Chatman were leaving quietly. The governor's speech had fallen over them like a pall. The room that had been filled with fun and gaiety was now electrified with fear.

Eva reluctantly said goodnight to Cecil. She trembled as his arm went around her shoulder and his voice betrayed his fear for her.

"I'm sure you're not still planning on going now," he said.

"I'll wait and see what this all means."

"The man just told you . . . 'blood will flow in the street.' That could be *your* blood."

"He also said the Guard will be there to protect us."

"That's not what he said. And even if he said that, do you believe him?"

"Aw, Cecil. I'll see what happens. Mrs. Floyd won't let us do anything that would harm us." She refused to see his frame of mind.

Cecil shrugged and sighed. "See you tomorrow after football practice, okay?"

"Fine. Take care."

"No. *You* take care." He squeezed her hands.

She looked into his eyes. Her heart raced and her throat tightened. For a moment she struggled to hold back tears. In spite of trying to appear calm, her mind buzzed with the governor's words.

The room was too quiet when she reentered — a sharp contrast to moments before. What had they expected? A red-carpet welcome at Chatman? At least sanction? But now Cecil's words about the governor's speech had Eva confused. "Blood will flow . . . protect our citizens." What did that speech really mean?

Mrs. Floyd sat with the group, appearing as calm as usual. However, Eva felt an uneasiness unknown before in all the meetings they had shared. Was Mrs. Floyd scared, too?

Nevertheless, when Mrs. Floyd spoke her voice was strong and reassuring. "You heard the governor ask for a restraining order from Judge Pomeroy, and for your parents to keep you home until a more feasible plan can be worked out. Now, I know the final decision must be made with you and your parents, but I would like to know what you all are thinking."

Eva looked from one face to another trying to figure if they all were as scared as she. Her mind kept wandering back to her father sitting with the shotgun. What if so many came that he would be outnumbered. They would all die. She shuddered at that thought.

Her mind refused to follow what was being said. It took great effort and a constant reminder to herself — pay attention.

"What if the judge does not agree with the governor? . . . Will we still have to go?" Harold asked.

"You will not *have* to go," Mrs. Floyd said. "You would still have the choice."

"A choice to get beaten up?" Lillian asked. They all laughed but tension was not relieved.

"Some choice," Arthur said.

"Didn't you hear the man?" Eva asked. "He said the soldiers were here to protect property and citizens."

"That's a good point, Eva," Mrs. Floyd said.

"But can we believe they'll see us as citizens?" Harold asked.

"If the courts tell us to go, they'll have to," Bobbie said.

"Let's wait," Mrs. Floyd said, "until the judge has made his decision; and we'll see what our lawyers think and what your parents think. . . ."

". . . And what we think," several people said at once, including Eva.

"Do you still think you want to go?"

Mrs. Floyd's question brought Eva back to the basic fear. Deep down under she still wanted to go but now she was afraid, not only for her father and family, but for herself.

"What about you, Eva?" Mrs. Floyd asked.

Eva had not heard what the others had said. She was on her own, and she said, "Yes, if the soldiers are there to protect us."

"Then if the judge says you are to go with the protection of the soldiers, all of you are still willing?"

They all agreed.

"Good, God bless you. We'll come together as soon as we get some of these answers."

"Are we going tomorrow, still?" Eva asked.

"The judge probably won't act until tomorrow. But we follow directions from the school's superintendent. If any word comes from him tonight, I'll let you know."

Parents arrived and everyone had gone except Eva. Eva had expected her father to be later than others because he had the farthest to come. But she had not thought he would be that late. She tried to settle down and not worry. The governor's words still controlled her thoughts and made her restless.

"What if they don't let us go, Mrs. Floyd?" she asked.

"We'll just keep on trying."

"Don't you ever get tired?"

"Can't get tired. For every gain, we sometimes might have to knock on twenty doors before one opens up to us. So we gear ourselves up to keep on knocking until one opens. And one *will*, eventually."

"Will it, Mis' Floyd?"

Mrs. Floyd reached over and patted Eva's hand. "Honey, I have faith. And that's the meaning of hope."

The doorbell rang. Eva jumped, startled. "Whew, I'm getting nervous."

"I wouldn't've been so late, but the street's crowded with outta state cars. I had t' go outta the way t' git here!" Her father came in, apologizing.

"Oh, that's all right. I enjoyed Eva's company," Mrs. Floyd said.

"I guess y' know the soldiers camped out 'round the school. . . . People in the streets goin' t' look at that."

"I hope you don't have any trouble going home. And don't you worry one bit about being late getting here."

Eva rode beside her father, sensing the danger they were in. They could be followed, forced off the road, even shot at before they got home. Only the sound of the motor interrupted their silence.

Her father knew every street in Mossville and several routes to their house. Now they took only side streets driving with their lights out. Slowly, slowly they made their way home.

Would they ever get home through those dark side streets? Eva leaned forward, her body willing them home.

Just as they neared the turn-off on the road leading into their section of town, a car came up behind them. Her father speeded up and turned. The car followed. Headlights glared in their rear-view mirror.

Cold sweat rolled down Eva's sides. She looked

at her father. He kept his eyes fixed on the road. They were almost home.

Suddenly the car cut around them with the horn blowing. "Turn on your lights, Roger," someone shouted.

Eva and her father laughed with relief. They had been followed by a friend. Her father turned on the lights and drove home safely.

The house was dark, but her mother met them at the door. She breathed a great sigh and said, "Thank God, I thought y'all would never git here."

"Blood will flow in the streets." The radio news used those words again and again. Eva sensed her mother's fear as she watched her pace up and down from room to room.

"Did Aunt Shirley go home?" Eva asked.

"Yeah, and took Tanya, thank God. I'll be so glad when this is all over. Oh, Eva, I wish . . . I wish. . . ."

"Turn off that radio and don't listen. That's nothin' but confusion," her father said.

"How we gonna know if we don't listen?" her mother asked.

"We heard what the governor said with our own ears. That is just a rehash and a lotta hearsay," her father said. "Let's now wait for the word of the judge."

"Mrs. Floyd said she will come and tell us any change in news, Mama. Try to calm yourself. Everything is all right," Eva said.

"Oh, you and your daddy. I just wish you two wasn't so stubborn."

"You call it stubborn, Mama, some people call it hopeful."

"Like a bee buzzing 'round a tar bucket," her mama said.

"Oh, Mama," Eva cried in anguish.

"Baby, I didn't mean it like that. But I'm scared and worried. How do we know if them soldiers here to do a job *for* us, or *on* us?"

"We'll have to see what the judge says tomorrow, Mama. If it's not safe, I promise I won't go." All at once, Eva felt exhausted. "Let's go to bed. I just might have to go to school tomorrow."

She lay in bed listening to the crickets. A dog far away howled at the stars and the sound of neighbors' muffled voices floated through her window. Lying still, Eva tried to force sleep.

But sleep wouldn't come. She tossed and turned. She dozed, but awoke immediately with a start, her eyes having lost the sleepiness. A mockingbird sang trill after trill. Eva marveled at such a powerful sound coming from so small a throat.

Finally the heat drove her from her small bed. She stood in the window bathed in the light of the million stars and the song of the mockingbird. For a moment she felt a surge of joy. It was as though she were one with the stars and the bird's song. Nothing else mattered. Oh, what peace! But it lasted only for a moment.

Then she thought of Grandma Collins and how she had known peace and happiness with her. But that was before she knew that drugstore ice cream could be as good, or better, than that made at home.

When had she learned that? She could not remember the exact time or place. Nor when she had learned that she was *different* and that the difference was measured only by color. She did not know when she had learned that no matter what she did she could not overcome that difference for she could not shed her skin. But she knew that after knowing, her world changed. She learned to be comfortable with herself and to expand within those boundaries of her dark hue. It was like attaining the security in learning to read a map. Once you know, you can never get lost again.

The song ceased. Only the silent stars remained. The dark, hot night closed in on her and she longed for the peace of sleep. Back on her bed, Eva floated between sleep and wakefulness. Then she was in a place where doors were wide, tall, and strongly built with small windows too high up to peep through. She was going from door to door knocking — knocking wildly — feeling an urgency to get inside. But there were no answers. She became frantic, running from door to door, knocking as loudly as she could. Then just the sound of knocking seemed to be all around her, pushing through her window and beneath the door, raising her up. She started up. The knocking was at their front door.

Eva jumped out of bed. "Daddy, Daddy," she called. "Somebody's at our door."

When she entered the living room, her father was standing with the gun in his hand. He was about to open the door.

"No! No, Daddy, don't open the door," Eva shouted.

"It's me, Mr. Collins," a voice rang out.

"Who?" shouted her father.

"It's me, Mrs. Floyd."

Eva stood in the middle of the room shivering. Cold sweat poured off her, even though the night was hot.

Tension showed in her father's voice. "What is it this time o' night?"

"Tell Eva she is *not* to go tomorrow. Our lawyers and the superintendent will let us know when, after the judge has made his decision."

Oh, no, Eva thought, but she could not say a word. She listened until the sound of Mrs. Floyd's car was lost in the distance. "Poor Mrs. Floyd, out here this time of night," she said. Then Eva went back into her room.

She heard her father moving about and wondered what time it was. Just then the cuckoo clock struck two. She sighed, knowing there were still hours ahead for troubled sleep.

Chapter 12

The ringing telephone woke Sophia and stirrings below indicated the household was up and about. The news on the radio immediately recalled last night's shattering spectacle. Sophia turned over in anger, her throat and chest tightening.

A door closed below and the sound of Burt's car made Sophia look at the clock. Six-thirty. The morning news continued to spiral upward to her room, and even though she could not clearly understand all that was being said, she knew this morning was not a usual first day of school.

Again a door closed. Soon the sound of her father's car backing out of the driveway came simultaneously with a flash of light shimmering on her wall — a reflection of the sunlight on the moving car. Already the sun was fierce.

Sophia stretched, feeling she had not had a moment's sleep. She lay trying to understand her unexpected exhaustion. Never before on the eve of the beginning of school had she gone to bed so unhappy and awakened with such a bitter feeling, regretting the day.

She loved school, and always before she had looked forward to its opening, preparing days ahead what she would wear, with whom she would walk, and what the whole day would be like. But this morning, she had no rousing enthusiasm. She did not want to go.

A delightful aroma floated around the room as Sophia drifted between sleep and wakefulness. M-m-mm, she thought. She sprang up — waffles! All the hunger of yesterday forced her out of bed. Suddenly she felt a welling up of happiness. Ida was back.

Clad only in her pajamas, the trousers cut off to her thighs, she raced down the stairs, her hunger mounting. The pleasant aroma engulfed her as she drew closer to the closed kitchen door.

She burst through. "Good morning. Gee, I'm starved."

Her mother was sitting at the glass-topped table on the back porch adjoining the kitchen, writing on a small notepad. On the kitchen countertop, the old-fashioned, round waffle iron gleamed as steam from cooking waffles poured out of its sides. Atop the stove, crisp strips of bacon were placed on paper towels, with little bubbles of fat still waiting to be absorbed. The sun shone through the window reflecting on the yellow curtains, brightening the whole room. Everything was in place.

Ida was pressing a garment, her body positioned

with her face toward the back porch. Suddenly Sophia had a strange sense that she was seeing this room and Ida in it for the first time. Then she remembered Rod and what she had felt when Grit bolted. That feeling had been fear, but what she felt now was different. She was not only seeing Ida as she was at the moment, but as she had been over the years.

It was Ida who wiped up spills, kept their clothes clean, and cooked the best meals. It was Ida whose parties were always a success, and Ida who was there to nurse them through illnesses, and to share their trials and triumphs. Only once in twenty years had she refused to come in every day of the week. For that she was fired. A storm of fury swept the house when Sophia's father demanded that her mother call Ida back.

Now as Sophia stood there she looked at her mother, trying to see the woman who had resisted and lost, who finally, in tears had asked Ida to come back.

Just then, Ida turned and flashed a smile. "It's about time y' was up, lady."

Sophia looked into Ida's black, almond-shaped eyes and at her dark, smooth-skinned face with its chiseled nose and well-shaped mouth.

Why hadn't she seen this exotic beauty in Ida before? Suddenly she realized that she knew nothing at all about this woman who had been in their household ever since she could remember, intimately bound up in her life. Surely Ida must know everything about her. Again she thought of Rod.

How could it be that she had not really seen Rod before? But she had seen him. He was there, to her, in the same way Grit was there. The way the tack room, the reins, and saddle were there — for her use, for her convenience.

Is that the way it was with Ida, too? No. She would not see Ida as one of *them*. She would not be afraid. She stood still, trembling, telling herself straighten up, walk past Ida, sit down at the table, and act natural.

"I didn't sleep at all. I'm exhausted," she said falling into a chair at the table with her mother.

"Y' might be exhausted, but it sho' ain't from no lack of sleep," Ida said and laughed.

"You calling me a liar?" Sophia shot back. She saw the surprised look on Ida's face, but she didn't care. She knew there was no cause for the anger rising in her. Still she let it take control. "How'd you know whether or not I slept?"

"Y' was either sleep or playin' a mighty good game at it when I was in y' room this mornin'," Ida said matter-of-factly as she prepared a plate with waffles and bacon for Sophia.

"And what were you doing in my room?" Sophia asked angrily.

"I asked her to get your dress and press it," her mother said. "Now you behave yourself."

Ida set the plate before Sophia.

"I refuse to eat waffles without syrup," Sophia said without looking up.

When Ida placed the syrup on the table, she left the kitchen.

"You don't walk out while I'm talking to you," Sophia shouted after Ida.

"Sophia!" her mother said.

"Come back here this minute, Ida," Sophia screamed.

"Sophia, now stop that nonsense," her mother said softly but firmly, when it was clear Ida was not coming back.

"Who does she think she is, calling me a liar."

"What is wrong with you? Ida was in no way hostile to you."

A voice on the radio interrupted the music with a news bulletin:

> The superintendent of schools has announced that the nine Negro students scheduled to enroll at Chatman will not report this morning. I repeat . . . will *not* report. . . . All other students are expected to attend school as scheduled.

Sophia's anger left her no energy to hail the bulletin as good news. She was so overwhelmed the food turned her stomach, and she pushed away from the table, feeling weak. The stairs were difficult, but she made it to her room determined that if Ida were there she would invite her out.

Alone, she sat on her bed trying to understand what was happening to her. Her world was sharply divided between whites and coloreds. It had always been that way. It was supposed to be that way. "But why didn't I know it?" she asked aloud. Why didn't someone prepare me for all of this?

A knock on the door made her freeze. Her heart pounded and her palms were clammy with sweat. It's Ida. What will I say to her? *Don't let her in.* Finally she answered, "Yes."

"I brought your dress," her mother said. "May I come in?"

"Come on."

The soft white shantung skirt and brown chiffon blouse with large white dots were pressed to perfection. Sophia remembered how she had asked Ida to help her choose a dress for the first day of school. They had chosen that one, and Ida had not forgotten. Suddenly the anger returned in full force. Tossing the garments aside she said, "I'll not wear this today."

She charged into the closet to make another choice. Everything seemed out of place. The heat compounded her frustration and futility as she rummaged through the clothes. She breathed a sigh of relief when the door closed on her mother's departure.

It was now seven-thirty. Five outfits were scattered over the room and still she couldn't decide on one. Why am I acting this way, she asked herself as she picked up the outfit Ida had pressed. It was, by far, the nicest. Why not wear it? No, she told herself, flinging the skirt aside. *Ida must not be in control of my life. No longer will I be dependent on her.*

Finally, she settled upon a multicolored, striped cotton dress and rushed into the shower.

Later, as she hurriedly put on the dress, she remembered, to her dismay, it was much too long and too big. Cinching a belt tightly at her waist, she glanced at herself in the mirror. She hated the way she looked, but now she had no time to change.

As she did her hair, the phone rang. She thought of Arnold and grimaced.

"It's for you," her mother called.

Terribly excited, she almost tripped over her feet as she bounded down the stairs. It was Marsha. To avoid missing one another, they agreed to meet in the gym at first period.

Hurt and disappointed, she dashed up to her room. The face that looked back at her from the mirror did not invite a pleasant smile, but Sophia tried. It was no use. She concluded that if the way she looked and felt was any indication of what her day would be, she was doomed.

Sophia held her purse and notebook on her lap, as her mother maneuvered through the unusually crowded streets. Cars from out of state, mostly Louisiana and Mississippi, were everywhere. The heat was stifling and the glare from the bright sun hurt Sophia's eyes. Wet with sweat, she felt weak, not only from the heat but also from not having eaten. Yet the choking fullness, the lump in her throat, refused to go away.

Her mother kept her eye on traffic, looking calm and poised. The unbothered manner made Sophia uneasy; she wanted to scream at her mother, "Help me!" Instead she said, "I wish I never had to go to Chatman again."

"I know how you feel, dear. But I wish you wouldn't worry so."

That response gave Sophia courage. She detected no pity in her mother's attitude, but a feeling of alliance. She had expected some chastisement and was surprised but grateful that her mother understood.

"How can I help worrying?" she said, not looking at her mother.

"Your father is doing all he can to help the governor, legally, to avoid this."

"But what can be done?"

"Be patient, dear, at least until the judge announces his decision today. I have hope. I don't think he'd dare undo our way of life."

Her mother's words made her happy. There was still hope. And maybe the soldiers were there to protect them as Burt had said. Actually, who were the outsiders? She wished she could be sure.

By the time they came within two blocks of Chatman, traffic had slowed to a crawl. The heat in the car was unbearable. Sophia decided to walk. She was amazed by the crowds on the street leading to the school. Sophia had never seen so many people, even on days of the most popular school events.

Newsmen pushed in the crowd. National television crews, with cameras in hand, were all over the place. The crowd was tense but mostly quiet. As Sophia neared the building, she saw the soldiers spread in a line covering the front, their bayoneted rifles by their sides. Her heartbeat quickened and she flushed with anger.

A tap on her shoulder forced Sophia around. It was Burt. Beside him was a young man with a light, reddish-brown beard. His brown eyes twinkled as he smiled at Sophia.

Burt introduced her. She noticed the name, Per Laursen, Denmark News Service, on the badge the young man wore. When Burt announced the name, Sophia smiled and said, "Welcome to Mossville."

"Thanks," he said. "Knowing your brother, I guess it's safe to assume you're in accord with Negroes coming to your school."

Sophia looked at Burt. The beaming smile on his face when he had introduced her as his sister was still there. She wanted him to remain as proud of her as he seemed, standing beside this newsman from a foreign country. For the first time ever she felt ashamed of what she thought about Negroes coming to Chatman. But she would not lie. She gave a little laugh. "My brother always told me good newsmen *never* assume. They search for and find the facts."

"Give me the facts, Sophia," Per said, laughing.

"Ask my brother," she said and darted through the crowd into the well-guarded building.

Compared to the crowd outside, the building seemed deserted. Sophia suddenly felt sad and alone. What if the white students didn't come? She made her way toward the gym to meet Marsha. She recognized no one about. Where was everybody?

She thought of that crowd outside, of Burt and his foreign friend.

The shame she had felt when asked the question rose in her again. It was quickly replaced by anger. *Why should I be ashamed of not wanting them here?* Suddenly she saw Ida's face as it had been when Ida placed the syrup on the table. What was in that face? She tried to recall but could not. And what had Rod felt when Grit almost ran him down? Were they angry, hurt, humiliated? Rod had said nothing, as if the incident had never happened. Ida had only left the room.

Suddenly she was overwhelmed with the now-familiar feeling. She didn't know if it was shame or fear. The choking she had felt in the car returned.

Then her mother's words came to her. "Your father is doing all he can . . . the judge announces his decision . . . he'd dare not undo our way of life." She adjusted her purse and notebook in her arms and hurried to meet Marsha.

Registration booths, familiar faces of teachers, and the hustle and bustle of students trying to get their favorite classes aroused Sophia's enthusiasm. Here was the true spirit of Chatman and the beginning of a new school year.

Teachers, positioned behind signs bearing their specialities, greeted Sophia and she began to feel that headiness that comes to seniors who are treated with a certain respect. But where were Marsha and all the others? The crowd of students was thin, indeed.

Nevertheless, she had to fill her class card, so

she began the rounds. She was glad to be there early for she had no problems getting classes she wanted. How exciting to have Mr. Seaton, the drama teacher, express pleasure at having her register for his class. Maybe the year would be fun after all.

By eleven o'clock the crowd in the gym had thinned further. Sophia had all of her classes secured and was impatient because none of her friends were around. Finally, she decided to go home.

The crowd outside was still thick, and tension had mounted. Sophia was surprised to hear people grumbling that Negroes were inside and white students had been told not to come. Could that rumor explain why Marsha had not shown?

The crowd pushed and shoved. Newspeople were jostled and booed. The Guard was hassled. Uneasiness gripped Sophia as she waded through the crowd. She scanned faces looking for Burt, but she did not see him.

Finally, on the edge of the crowd, she decided to go to the corner drugstore to have a bite to eat. Just as she stepped off the walk to cross the street, she saw Arnold standing near the store's entrance. Her heart beat wildly and her first thought was to run in another direction. But before she could move, he had waved and was coming toward her.

A rush of heat started in her stomach and moved up spreading to the top of her head. Suddenly she was aware of herself and how she must look; dress too long and big, face red under the freckles. Why hadn't she worn the outfit Ida had pressed for her?

She wished she could disappear. Then Arnold was there in front of her.

"Hello, Sophia," he said.

The familiar ring of his voice and the warm smile tied her tongue. She stood looking at him. He seemed not to notice her inability to speak.

"I called several times yesterday. Did you go away with your family some place?"

She finally found her voice. "No . . . we didn't go away at all."

"Sophia, I called at noon, again at three and at six. No one was home."

"Oh, yeah, I took Grit out and then I went skating."

"And I thought you'd be missing me. I'm leaving Thursday, you know. I want to talk to you!"

For a moment she panicked. Then warmth returned and she could feel calm settling over her. He had called three times; had wanted to see her.

She looked up, needing to say how much she had missed him. How unhappy she had been because she had been rude to him. But the words would not come. So, she took his hand and said, "I did miss you, and I want to talk to you, too."

Together they entered the store on the corner.

Chapter 13

Sophia was holding on to Arnold's hand. The strong smell of corn liquor, tobacco, and stale body sweat, mixed with that of frying food and the heat, made her stomach turn.

All eyes were on her as a female when she entered. Her quick glance took in the tense, angry men who looked like those she had seen riding up and down streets around town. Sophia flushed, feeling uneasy.

Arnold steered her to a small booth where she finally placed an order. They did not talk, Sophia sensing that Arnold was as ill-at-ease as she with this crowd in their work overalls and wide soft-brimmed hats, some of felt, most of straw. The quiet of the place also bothered Sophia. She felt that she was bound together with these strangers in an act of waiting. But waiting for what? She shyly glanced around. There were no answers in those faces. But suddenly she knew that those men were all of one mind, one will, and given a signal they would jump to any action, good or evil. She shuddered.

"Bloodthirsty bunch, eh?" Arnold asked, sensing her thoughts.

She lowered her head and whispered, "Golly, I'd hate to have them against me."

Even though she was hungry, she picked at her ham sandwich and slowly sipped lemonade.

Finally Arnold said, "I'm having to leave just when things are getting exciting in this town. I've never seen so many newsmen in so small a place."

"I met one all the way from Denmark this morning."

"Met him?"

"Yeah. Per Laursen. I have connections, you know."

"Must be nice to have a brother like Burt."

"Comes in handy sometimes."

"Oh, I don't just mean having him as a news reporter."

"Aw, he's all right."

"I think he's one of the greats in this town even though he's not quite thirty."

"You would think that." Sophia blurted out.

"Well, don't you?"

Be cautious, she told herself. Don't ruin this moment. "He's my brother," she said and grinned.

Arnold laughed. "That's no answer to my question, Sophia."

"Please, let's leave it at that, okay?" She reached across and placed her hand over his.

The strange men were gradually replaced by more familiar faces as students came into the place. Then there was lots of talk and laughter. Marsha and the whole gang arrived. Sophia immediately thought of the pact. She didn't want Arnold to know about it, so she turned away from the entrance and lowered her eyes.

"Your friends," Arnold said.

She was of a mind to deny them and say let's go. But the place was too small to escape unnoticed. In no time she was discovered and surrounded. Marsha and Lisa squeezed in beside Sophia, Meredith in beside Arnold. The others stood about.

"Why weren't you at the gym like you said?" Sophia asked.

"I tried calling you back, but you'd gone already," Marsha said. "Sorry 'bout that, but I see your time was not wasted." She nodded toward Arnold and winked at Sophia.

"No. I got all the classes I wanted with no sweat. Hardly anybody I knew was there."

"How can that be? We were told there was no school, eh, Lisa?"

"Who told you that?" Sophia asked.

"Meredith called me," Lisa said.

"And who told Meredith?" Sophia turned her attention to Meredith whose pink cotton quilted skirt took up a lot of space with its white ruffled petticoats. The sight of Meredith's skirt and the cool pink, cotton voile blouse, trimmed in dainty white lace, made Sophia flush. The flush spread as she looked down at her too long, too big, striped dress remembering the nice skirt and blouse she had left crumpled on her bed. "Meredith. . . ."

". . . and where have you been that I've not met

you before?" Meredith was asking Arnold as Sophia called her name.

"I might ask you that," Arnold said looking at Meredith with a warm smile.

Sophia swallowed hard trying to stop the knot at her throat but it spread, leaving her scarlet and speechless under Meredith's cold stare.

Marsha rescued Sophia when she said, "He's been busy with Sophia."

"Oh," Meredith put a hand to her strangely attractive hairdo and widened her blue eyes. "Where I come from boys and girls aren't that busy unless, of course, they're engaged."

"We really haven't had enough time, and I'm leaving the day after tomorrow," Arnold said and touched Sophia's hand.

"How exciting," Meredith said. "Take me with you."

"Ha!" Sophia laughed. "Where I come from a girl wouldn't dare ask a fellow she didn't know to take her away with him, especially if she didn't know where he was going." Sophia stood up. "Excuse me, y'all. Arnold, I think we'd better go."

"We just got here, Sophia," Marsha said. "Don't go."

"Yeah, stay. Let's goof off a bit. This might be our last chance, you know," Kim said.

"Remember tomorrow," Lisa said and quickly placed her hands over her ears, eyes, and mouth.

Everybody started giggling and making the symbols.

"What's that all about?" Arnold asked.

"Oh, that's our. . . ."

"No!" Sophia shouted at Meredith. "Only seniors. Remember what we said now." Quickly she collected herself and smiled. "Really, I must go." She took Arnold's hand and started out. She stopped, made the symbol, and waved good-bye. She left laughing.

"What's with hands over ears, eyes, and mouth?" Arnold asked as soon as they were outside.

"You're still not a senior, Arnold Armstrong," she said, hugging his arm closely.

"Well, I won't worry. One can't go too far wrong with those symbols: seeing no evil, hearing no evil, and speaking no evil, right?" He looked at her and smiled.

"Right," she said. What a narrow escape, she thought as she recalled Meredith's attempt to tell Arnold about the pact. And who had told Meredith that there was no school, she wondered. Again she felt the coldness of the stare Meredith had given her. Suddenly she was aware of the same uneasiness in her thoughts about Meredith that she had felt with those tense, rough men who were now crowding the sidewalks around Chatman.

Chapter 14

Eva's day had begun with the sound of Mr. Charles's old rooster crowing. Eva lay still, listening to the morning sounds. In her mind's eye she saw the clucking hens lazily tumbling off the roost, their wings slightly spread. Suddenly she was wide awake, her mind full of Mrs. Floyd's late visit and the thought of no school for her today. How could the governor do such a thing? Why have the troops, if they were not there to get them into school?

She sat up on the side of her bed trying to close her mind to all thought. No use. Her mind zigzagged from one thing to another, leaving her confused. Never in her life had she missed a first day of school. Always the excitement of going had built up over the days to a point where, on the night before, she could not sleep. The morning found her the first up, getting ready to go. What if the judge says we can't go to Chatman — ever? She must not think of that. It would be a long wait for his Decision.

She went to the clothes closet, took out her black and white dress and spread it on Tanya's bed.

Quickly she placed her new socks and black-and-white saddle shoes near the dress. Stepping back, with one hand on her hip, the other on her chin, she surveyed the results. Neat, she thought and smiled. But her mind was immediately clouded — no school.

Quietly she put the things away and lay on her bed trying to fight the sadness welling up inside. Stirrings of her father who was an early riser aroused her. She threw on her robe and went into the kitchen.

"Morning, Daddy."

Already her father had started breakfast. His hands were covered with flour. He answered her with a quiet greeting. "Mornin'. What y' doin' up so early?"

"Couldn't sleep. Old first-day-of-school routine, I guess."

"Good habit, I would say."

Eva sat at the end of the small table where her father worked. His long slender fingers deftly handled dough that would finally be shaped into the best biscuits she had ever eaten. Her father was as good a cook as his sister, Shirley. He thought she was the best. Aunt Shirley's biscuits were so rich they were not even called biscuits. They were called *scones*.

Her father's face was drawn this morning and Eva knew he was sad and worried, too. She should have left him to find peace in the early morning sounds as he worked that dough to his satisfaction.

But she needed to be near him and the doubts buzzing in her head wanted quieting in conversation.

Finally, she spoke, trying to control the urgency she felt. "Daddy, you think the judge will let us go tomorrow?"

Not looking up, her father answered, "The good Lord don't tell his business to nobody, and me and the judge ain't on no speaking terms, so I can truthfully say, I don't know."

Eva laughed. "Oh, Daddy, I asked what do you think?"

He looked up at her and smiled. "Oh, I think he will; and if wishin' made it so, you'd be goin' this mornin'."

The smile lifted his face and Eva felt a warm glow. She knew her father loved her and would do all in his power to make her happy.

"Now, Missy," he said as he placed the pan of biscuits in the oven, "you fry some bacon and scramble some eggs and we'll be in good shape by the time these biscuits git brown."

It was still early morning when Eva saw her mama and daddy off to the store. Sounds of children calling back and forth held Eva at the front door. She watched the children collect friends and saunter off to school dressed in their best, heralding the day. Tanya would be leaving from Aunt Shirley's.

Already it was hot, the sun brilliant in a high silvery sky. The children's calling and the sound of the old cotton gin were the only indications that fall was near and that today was the opening of school.

For the first time in her life, Eva heard these sounds without sweet excitement and the rush of joy.

What if there is no school for me? The thought frightened her. School was everything. It was the end of long, hot uneventful days . . . the beginning of planned fun and challenging things. Most of all it meant books and reading again after an almost bookless summer. What would she do if there were no school library?

Her mind flashed to the big library downtown. She had heard there were thousands of books in that building. Rooms filled with them. She didn't know, for no Negroes were allowed in that library to read or borrow books. *Oh, the things she couldn't do.* But she must not think of that.

The sounds of the children faded and quiet settled on the street and in her house. She felt restless. If only she knew what that judge would decide. She could always go back to Carver. She moved through the quiet house, wishing she had gone to the store with her mom and dad.

She spent a long time under the shower wondering how she could pass the day. Maybe she should take the bus and go over to Bobbie's. *No.* Maybe she should take the bus to her Aunt Shirley's. But she wanted to be near when the Decision came. She decided the store was the best place.

As she searched for something cool to wear, she again pulled out her new dress. She would press it some more, and make sure every seam was open, every loose thread tied and clipped.

Just as she was done and putting away the ironing board, she heard a knock at the door and a call, "Eva, you home?"

It was Bobbie. "Hi, girl, what you doing over here?"

"I came to get you. Let's go to Carver and see what's happening."

"You think we should go there today?"

"Why not?"

"Oh, girl, they might make us feel . . . you know . . . they might laugh at us."

"Who cares? Come on."

"I don't know if I want to."

"I want to do something," Bobbie said walking up and down the room. "Girl, I'm so nervous and jumpy. I gotta get away from that news."

"We didn't listen this morning, and I'm glad."

"I wish we hadn't. Those crazy people milling 'round Chatman thinking we there. Ain't that stupid?"

"Bobbie, you think they'll ever let us go?"

"I don't know, girl, after all of this, I'm getting scared."

"You *can't* be scared. Girl, you're my support, my buddy."

"I know," Bobbie said.

"I'm just hoping that judge will hurry up and say yes. Then everything will be okay with the soldiers there to protect us."

"Come on, let's go to Carver and forgit Chatman."

On the way Eva sensed the tension in the neighborhood. On street corners and on porches small knots of people gathered, talking about the troops and about all the out-of-state cars roaming around town. There were rumors of Negroes being pulled from buses and rocks thrown into their cars.

"Why so many people not working today?" Eva asked as they went on their way.

"People can't get across town. I tell you, they acting crazy down there around Chatman."

Suddenly Eva thought of the talk about bombings. "Maybe we never should have tried to go to Chatman in the first place. Getting outta place."

"Girl, I'm beginning to think maybe. . . ."

"But Bobbie, somebody had to. I'm scared, but I'm glad, too. If only that old governor hadn't stepped in and said no."

The old fear returned and the closer they came to Carver, the more Eva felt that she could not face the students and the teachers. She certainly did not want to see Cecil, not knowing when she would be going to school again. What could she say? She felt ashamed that she was not at Chatman.

Suddenly she stopped. "Bobbie, I can't, I can't go to Carver now." She turned and started back.

"Eva, what's wrong with you?" Bobbie called after her.

Eva knew she could not explain what she was feeling and make Bobbie understand. She didn't know herself why she should feel ashamed to go to Carver. "You go on. I might come later, but I can't go there now." She decided to go to the store. News of the judge's Decision would reach the store more quickly than at any other place she could go.

* * *

When she reached the store her mother was busy with customers and her father was out. Not wanting to talk, Eva went straight to the back. Absentmindedly she moved papers around on her father's desk, wishing news of the judge's Decision would hurry up and come. "Oh Lord, please don't let him say we can't go," she prayed silently.

She went back up front. All the customers had been waited upon and her mother was now looking at a magazine.

"I'm glad you're here, Eva. I was worried, wondering how you'd spend the day."

"I started to go to Carver. . . ." She wanted so much to tell her mother about the feeling of shame, but she could not find the words. "I thought I'd come help out here instead."

"We can always use help here, but maybe it'd be best if y' went there . . . be with y' friends."

"No. Where's Daddy?"

"At the wholesale house."

"I'll help awhile. Maybe I'll go to Carver later."

Eva stood for a minute listening to music on a small radio. "Any news?" she finally asked.

"Nothin' new. Crazy people still crowdin' round lookin' at the soldiers. They really mad. They don't like nothin' that might help us," her mother said and sighed.

Her mother's tone increased Eva's fear that she wouldn't be going to school. She went in back and got busy. As she placed cans of tomato paste on the shelf she was glad she had decided to come to work. Time would go by faster this way.

She went on stacking cans, her mind wandering back and forth. She tried to forget the shame she felt about going to Carver. Did she really dislike Carver? Would she be unhappy if she had to go back? No. Suddenly she felt a pang of guilt for thinking such thoughts. She liked her school, had been happy there and was not anxious to leave. Then why be ashamed to go there? Forget it, she told herself. It's all crazy. Still she could not shake the feeling.

Then the news came on the radio.

The president of the local school board has called a meeting of its members to stand by for Judge Pomeroy's desegregation decision. That decision — to determine if the nine Negroes will enroll at Chatman High School tomorrow — should come at any moment now.

Eva's heart pounded as she hurried up front. "Mama, Mama," she shouted, "did you hear that?"

Before her mother could answer, her father and Mrs. Floyd rushed into the store.

"Mis' Floyd," Eva shouted.

Mrs. Floyd hugged Eva and choked up with tears. For a moment the silence was almost unbearable for Eva. Finally, Mrs. Floyd said, "We won, Eva."

"Oh, no!" Eva screamed.

"Oh, yes, yes, yes!" Mrs. Floyd said. "You can·

go tomorrow. I'm making the rounds telling every-body. Just make sure now, you and Bobbie get to-gether in the morning."

"You say it's all go now, eh?" Eva's mother asked.

"Yes, when we were told Judge Pomeroy's De-cision, we were assured that the soldiers will pro-tect us as we uphold the law."

Everybody was hugging each other, eyes were wet with tears of joy. Eva was so happy she couldn't contain herself. "Now that I'm going to Chatman, I'm going to Carver," she said, and ran out the door.

On the way she felt her heart would burst with happiness. She wanted to shout out to everyone she met . . . to the whole world, we won! But she just went on her way smiling, radiating happiness.

She entered the campus grounds and realized it was well after four o'clock. No one was around. She hurried toward the football field. There was Cecil walking toward the gym, carrying his football hel-met in his hand.

She started running toward him. "Cecil, Cecil, Cec'," she shouted. "We won, we won, we won!"

He met her and she fell into his arms. He whirled her around and around as she continued to cry, "We won."

Finally they settled down. She was out of breath. "I'm going . . . tomorrow . . . to Chatman."

He stood watching her, sweat pouring off his gritty face. His football outfit was wringing wet and his face showed mixed emotions. At last he said quietly, "Great, great, great!"

"You think so?" she asked, subdued by this response.

"Yeah, I really do."

Then they were silent. Eva felt her heart race inside her chest, her breath coming too fast. She looked at Cecil. "Are you really glad I'm going?" Then she lowered her head.

"Oh, Eva, how could I not be happy? We really have a choice now. All before, I didn't really know whether or not my wanting to stay here was just sour grapes. Now I know. I can do what I please. I can go or I can stay."

He took her chin in his hand and lifted her face so that she looked him in the eyes. "You're giving us that choice." For a moment they were silent looking at each other. Finally he laughed, "Maybe I'm a little bit jealous. I would like to be giving that choice to you."

Her mind flashed to her grandmother and the drugstore ice cream. Suddenly she knew why she had been ashamed to come to Carver before the Decision. She could not face being a symbol of their having lost the first round. In spite of the grime and the sweat, she reached up and embraced Cecil.

He held her close and whispered, "I'm glad but, you know, I can't believe we've won."

"I'm so glad *you're* glad," she said.

Sophia entered the coolness of her house feeling she had had a good day. It had started off bad with Ida, gone through a positive change when her mother had given her hope that Judge Pomeroy was an honest sensible man, and it had continued to improve with Arnold. Except for the thought that Arnold was leaving soon, she was happy.

She went through to the back of the house, feeling buoyant, calling, "Anybody home besides me?"

"We're back here, dear," her mother called from outside.

The kitchen was filled with good odors. Ida was frying chicken to go with mashed rutabagas, collard greens, and golden-brown corn bread. Sophia rushed through to the backyard where her parents were sitting in the shade. A small radio was on the table beside a pitcher that held the last of the sarsaparilla. She poured what was left into a glass and said, "Saw Burt today. He introduced me to a friend of his all the way from Denmark."

Before her news could be commented upon, more important information came on the radio:

Judge Pomeroy of the Ninth Circuit Court of Appeals has just issued this statement to the press: Believing that the governor is sincere in calling out the National Guard to protect citizens in this state, I see no reason to issue a restraining order against integration at Chatman High. Therefore, I instruct the school board to carry through with plans to enroll nine Negro students on September 5, 1957.

"Daddy, you knew it. You knew it all the time and you wouldn't tell me," Sophia screamed.

Her father and mother looked at her, startled by her outburst.

"I will not go to that school ever again. I refuse!" she shouted, feeling her heart pounding in her chest.

"Listen to me, young lady," her father said, "if you remain in this household you'll obey the law. . . ."

"But Daddy. . . ."

"Now you listen. I promise you, I'll do all within my power to change that law. But as long as that *is* the law, you'll obey it. Is that clear?"

"You may make me go to that school, but, I tell you, I will see no *niggers*, hear no *niggers*, and I will speak to no *niggers*!" Her heart seemed hushed as the words found their mark. She saw the look on her father's face, and knew her world was shattered. She covered her face and ran from the backyard.

Chapter 15

The sun rose hot that September 5, 1957, a morning different from any morning Eva had known. Though she had not gone to bed until well after midnight, she was up early feeling the exciting pressures of the day ahead. At last she was going to Chatman.

All last evening sparked by TV cameras and newsmen around the store and at the house, neighbors and friends dropped in to celebrate the victory of the great Decision.

Eva's mother and Aunt Shirley had hurriedly prepared cookies and lemonade for the party that lasted on into the night. Those going and coming filled the small house with talk and laughter. The fears that had been so evident earlier that day seemed to have dissolved with the declaration of the judge that the soldiers were there to protect citizens. To Eva's neighbors and friends that meant *them*, too.

Eva had gone to bed happy, listening to Tanya's even breathing. She was pleased that her family was all together and had shared the loyalty of neighbors and friends.

Now, as she dressed carefully, she could hear voices and knew her neighbors were coming to see her off and wish her well on what they called her "historic mission." She spread lotion over her body being especially careful to cover her exposed arms and legs. She must look her best when she walked on that campus this morning.

How pleased she was when she surveyed herself in the dress she had made. The new shoes and socks made her feel that she was very well dressed, indeed.

Finally, she walked into her living room. She was surprised to see so many of her neighbors gathered around waiting for her to come out. There were greetings and smiles and Eva knew they were as excited and as proud of her as her family.

"Now, I hope y' had a good breakfast," Mr. Charles said.

"Ain't that the truth, 'cause she got a day comin' up," another neighbor said.

"And she didn't half eat this morning," her mother said.

"Too much else happenin' t' be thinkin' 'bout food," Aunt Shirley said.

Her father quietly paced back and forth. Eva knew he was nervous thinking about that crowd that was still milling around Chatman.

Finally, it was time for her to go.

"Eva, I'm goin' take y'," her father said.

"No, Daddy. You don't need to go. I'm going to

meet Bobbie on the bus. The bus will put us off right in front of the school. We'll be all right."

"I know y' can git the bus, but I'll feel much better takin' y' up there m'self."

"You really don't need to get in all that traffic, Daddy."

"I don't want nothin' t' happen t' you."

"What can happen? We'll get off the bus and meet the others. The bus stops right in front of the school. The soldiers are right there."

"Now Roger, y' know how it is when y' fifteen," Aunt Shirley said. "Y' don't want y' papa takin' y' to school. She should be safe."

"Lord, let's hope so," a neighbor said. "Nobody would want to hurt a child."

"Yeah, they'd be mo' 'en likely to git on you, Roger," another neighbor said. "She'll be all right. Specially with them soldiers right there."

"Eva, what if you miss Bobbie, though?" Aunt Shirley asked.

"Aw, please. Stop worrying! Anyway, the soldiers are there to protect us."

Her mother looked at Eva as if she wanted to speak but she said nothing. She picked up her daughter's notebook and small purse and handed them to Eva.

Just as Eva started to go, her mother said, "Wait." She put a hand on Eva's shoulder. "I want all y'all to join me in prayer for my child."

Eva glanced around the room feeling the concern of all the bowed heads. She then bowed her head as her mother prayed: "God, our Father, kind and jus' who work y' ways through *us*, Father, let only good come to this child as she got out there t' do *your* will. Bless Eva. . . ." Her mother's voice choked with unshed tears.

Eva embraced her mother, trying hard to fight the choking in her own throat. "I'll be all right, Mama. I'll meet Bobbie. I'll be fine, you'll see."

She waved good-bye to her family and neighbors and walked down the hot dusty road to catch the bus. She turned and looked back. Her father was standing with an arm around her mother's shoulder with Tanya in front of them. She had an urge to go back and embrace them all as her heart leaped up with love. But she went quickly on her way.

Chapter 16

The sun had burned all the blue out of the sky. It blazed hot and chose the town as its prey. The heat beat down as with a vengeance. But in spite of the heat, cars poured into the street. Horns blowing in the snarled traffic heightened the tension.

The best laid plans were mislaid. The whole town was off schedule.

Bobbie was warned to stay home by telephone, but when the traffic crawled to a halt, Mrs. Floyd was caught. She did not reach Eva in time, even though the Southend bus was forty minutes late.

Burt let Sophia off a block from the school. When she turned the corner, she was shocked at the number of people in the blazing heat. More than yesterday.

Angry men, women, and children faced the soldiers who stood in a line guarding the steps — like the lion. The soldiers stood with feet apart, holding their rifles with bayonets fixed at their sides. The people did not know why the soldiers were there at the foot of the steps, so they believed they were against them. The soldiers looked straight ahead as the crowd taunted, "Hey, y' skin might be white, but y' heart's yeller."

Sophia looked up at her school. The three-story red brick building with massive white columns and long flight of steps leading up to its doors looked too grand to be part of this scene. But the stone lion at the foot of the steps seemed to assure Sophia that all would be well. She edged along the rear of the crowd, pausing when the heat and smell of stale sweat made her weak.

Finally she saw Marsha off in the direction of the bus stop. Sophia pushed along, sickened by the press of grubby hands and bodies. Still she felt a high excitement she could not define.

At last she reached Marsha. Meredith and Kim had gotten there, too.

"They're inside," Meredith declared angrily. "They've invaded our school."

Marsha stood absentmindedly tearing a dainty handkerchief to shreds. Tears were rolling down her cheeks. Sophia placed an arm around Marsha's shoulder and glared at the Guard, wishing some power would blow them away.

Suddenly there was a shout. "Here comes one of 'em." An angry rumbling spread through the crowd. The mass seemed to move in a wave, pushing Sophia and her friends closer to the bus stop. Sophia saw the Southend bus pull away. Then she saw the Negro. How dare she come here, Sophia thought. *And alone!* She trembled with anger.

The crowd parted to let the girl through. She moved with her head slightly lowered. Carrying a notebook and a small purse in her arms, she walked confidently toward the soldiers.

For a moment all was quiet. The waiting silence made Sophia feel that, in that moment, the girl held the crowd's destiny in her dark hands.

Eva walked on, believing the Guard, there to protect her, would let her enter the building. But as she got near the stone lion, the soldiers lifted their rifles and tightened their line, blocking her way.

Eva darted to get through another opening in the ranks, but just as quickly the ranks closed and she found herself facing bayonets. She was bewildered.

A roar went through the crowd. Now they knew! *The guard was on their side!* Boldly someone shouted, "Git going, *nigger*."

Eva became frightened, lost her confidence, and floundered. She looked at the soldiers, then turned toward the angry, churning mob. She panicked as one caught between a raging fire and a snake-infested river.

Sophia couldn't believe the looks on the faces of the men, women, and children. Their faces were contorted masks as they howled, hissed, and screamed at the girl.

She's trapped! Sophia thought, hugging herself for safety.

"Oh, God, help me," Eva prayed. "Show me a way out of no way." Suddenly she remembered the bench by the bus stop. She must make it there. She moved with the mob at her heels, her head high, her shoulders straight. The crowd closed in behind her, but she knew not to run. The howling continued to follow her as she moved along, just a few steps in front of the crowd. Suddenly she slowed, her head lowered, her shoulders drooped. Eva continued to pray, "Oh, heavenly Father, don't forsake me now. Let me not hear; let me not see; let me not feel a thing. Move with me to that bench."

What is she ever going to do? Sophia wondered as the girl came closer to her and the bus stop. When the girl reached the bench, the mob pressed in, pushing Sophia away from her friends.

Then Meredith rushed to the girl and spat in her face. And the spit rained down.

For a moment Sophia stood stunned. The shame and the fear she had known for days returned full force. She felt helpless as the people heaped abuse on the Negro girl. She couldn't believe the crowd was human. The heat and stench of angry bodies almost overwhelmed her. She wanted to escape, but she turned again to look at the girl.

Eva was about to cry.

Sophia covered her mouth to stifle a scream. She was suffocating, pushing through the crowd. For a moment darkness, then she was on the bench, whispering urgently, "Don't cry! Please, don't let them see you weaken. If you break now, they'll kill you."

Then the spit hit Sophia.

"Nigger lover!" Sophia looked up into Meredith's

eyes as the words they'd chosen to curse one worse than a traitor rang out again and again. Even Marsha joined in the screaming.

Sophia felt nothing but urgency to get away. "Please call a taxi," she shouted. No one responded. If only they could make it to the drugstore. The owner knew Sophia. There she could phone for help. But who? The police were off limits, the Guard was in control. But just maybe the police, if called.

"Come on, let's try to get out," Sophia said, pulling Eva up from the bench, shielding her with her body as best she could.

They clung to each other and stumbled along, and somehow they reached the drugstore, only to have the door slammed shut in their faces.

The angry crowd followed them back to the bench, taunting and cursing. Their words did not bother Sophia. She was worried about the girl who had not uttered a sound: It was as if her spirit moved in a dead body.

Finally a city bus came. Somehow they got aboard, and the driver sped away.

The girl sat in shock, and Sophia worried that she might never speak again. Alarmed, she asked, "Where do you want to go?"

There was no answer. Sophia waited. Gradually the numbness in her body ebbed. Her clothes were covered with spit. She wanted to tear those clothes off. Then she looked at the girl bathed in spit. The girl sat as though she wanted nothing to touch her body, not even her own hands or arms. Sophia turned away, sick with shame.

Finally, she took the girl's hand, saying, "I want to take you home."

Eva looked at Sophia. "Why you?" she asked.

The undertone of suspicion and anger surprised Sophia, but she remembered her friends. Their screams of *"nigger lover"* rang in her ears. She had no answer. Yes, she thought, why me?

"You're the one who made me wait in Woolworth's, remember?"

"Oh, my Lord," Sophia cried. Why hadn't she recognized this tall bronze girl who, only four days before, had stood before her, calm and composed, with three little items in her hand. Suddenly she flushed with shame and said, "My name is Sophia Stuart. What's your name?"

"Eva . . . Eva Collins. I want to know, why you? I really want to know."

Sophia said, "I don't know why. I can't tell you why. But I do know, at the time, I was not helping you. I was helping myself. It was as if I was drowning, forcing myself up for air . . . and here we are."

"Yeah . . . here we are," Eva said. "Thank you." She folded into herself again.

The bus driver picked up passengers at each stop. Finally one boarded who, in horror and great pity, recognized Eva and knew where she should go. Sophia went with him to take her there.

Chapter 17

News flashed around the world that the Guard in the town of Mossville had turned bayonets on Eva Collins, a fifteen-year-old Negro girl, forcing her to face an angry mob. And that Sophia Stuart, a charming Southern young lady from a staunch Mossville family, had assisted the girl. . . .

Sophia listened to the television news and wanted to believe that she was a charming young lady, but then she remembered the looks on the faces of her friends, the ugly words they had hurled at her; the look on her mother's face when she had come home, and the words, "Oh, we're ruined!"

Now Sophia looked at her mother and wondered, How can she be so angry at me? So frozen? Thank God for Ida, she thought. Ida had had the good sense to take me into the backyard, hose me off, strip me down, and help me clean myself.

She glanced sideways at her father, who sat with his hands wedged between his knees, intent on the television.

Then she looked at Burt and lowered her eyes,

thinking, What have I done to them?

Finally her mother said, *"Charming lady.* . . . Oh, Sophia, I wish it were so, but . . . oh, why did this happen to us?" These same words had been said over and over since first she heard the news.

"Maybe it's my fault, stressing that she must obey the law," her father said. "But I had no idea she'd go out and insist on others obeying!"

"I didn't insist on anybody," Sophia said, remaining calm.

"Please. Let's not lay blame," Burt said. "If you ask me, I'll say she's charming, a lady in the *true* sense of the word."

Sophia looked at her mother. She could hear the angry, abusive voices of that mob, and suddenly she realized her parents were not as much angry as they were afraid. She felt a rush of love for them as the words tumbled out of her. "I did what I had to do. I don't know why, but I did. And if what I have done is so disastrous, then the disaster is *mine."*

Her words hung on the silence. A sudden shiver seized her, as if a warm security blanket had been snatched away and she was exposed to a cold, blinding light. But her world was slowly turning right side up again, and she was beginning to see things clearly. She glanced from one face to the other. Again she remembered Marsha, Kim, and Meredith, and she knew. She wanted the love of her family and the respect of her friends, but she no longer needed to see the world as they saw it. She looked at Burt and smiled. What she had gained was the beginning to the end of her pain.

Author's Note

On May 17, 1954, the United States Supreme Court changed the course of U.S. history in a reversal of the *Plessy* v. *Ferguson* decision of 1889. *Plessy* v. *Ferguson* upheld a Louisiana law requiring separate railway facilities for whites and people of African origin classified then as *colored*. Mr. Justice Brown announced the Court's opinion:

> . . . If one race be inferior to the other socially, the Constitution of the United States cannot put them on the same plane.

Thus was created the "separate but equal" doctrine, which adversely affected the lives of African-Americans socially, economically, and politically.

Sixty-five years later, in *Brown et al.* v. *Board of Education of Topeka et al.*, the *Plessy* decision was overturned. A unanimous verdict by the 1954 Court was read by Mr. Justice Warren:

. . . In the field of public education the doctrine of "separate but equal" has no place. Separate educational facilities are inherently unequal.

The Court mandated that school boards end school segregation "with all deliberate speed."

At the time of that decision, African-Americans were classified as *Negro*.

The 1954 decision raised the hopes and aspirations of Negroes, but they knew the law had little meaning until it was implemented. Therefore, the National Association for the Advancement of Colored People (NAACP) organized legal procedures to implement the Court's decision.

In September of 1957, a plan to integrate nine Negroes into Central High School in Little Rock, Arkansas, reached its final stages. The plan incensed some of the citizens. The governor of the state, Orval Faubus, called in the state's National Guard.

On September 4, an angry crowd gathered around the school to taunt the Guard and to thwart the plan. The purpose of the Guard was not clear until one of the nine students, Elizabeth Eckford, tried to enter the school. With bayonets fixed, the Guard denied her entrance. The crowd, seeing that the Guard was there to prevent integration, vented their anger on Elizabeth.

Elizabeth, unable to escape their abuse, sat on a bench at a bus stop near the school. The mob followed and drenched her with spit.

Grace Lorch braved the mob and sat beside Elizabeth. Mrs. Lorch was a nonsouthern white who taught with her husband, Lee, at Philander Smith College, an all-Black school in Little Rock. Subsequently, she shielded Elizabeth and helped her onto a city bus that went to the place where Elizabeth's mother worked.

The issue of state authority versus federal authority had to be settled. President Dwight D. Eisenhower federalized Arkansas's Guard and then sent troops from the 101st Airborn Division into the city. Under the protection of the troops the nine Black students entered Central High School on Wednesday, September 25.

The Girl on the Outside is a fictional re-creation of that incident. The courage of Grace Lorch, of the nine Black students, and of Mrs. Daisy Bates, the NAACP official who helped implement the plan, inspired my story.

About the Author

MILDRED PITTS WALTER was a teacher in the Los Angeles schools in the 1960s, and her husband, the late Earl Walter, was city chairman of CORE, the Congress of Racial Equality.

As members of CORE, they worked with the ACLU and the NAACP to initiate *Crawford* v. *Los Angeles Board of Education*, in 1968. They hoped this case would end segregation in their public school system.

She had long been inspired by Grace Lorch's courageous action during the 1957 desegregation crisis in Little Rock, Arkansas, and talked with many of the people involved before beginning this story, fictionalized to speak directly to teenagers about the problems they face in accepting integration.

Author of such books as *Ty's One Man Band* and *Lillie of Watts*, Mildred Pitts Walter is also an educational consultant who especially enjoys helping children develop their appreciation of Black culture. She lives in Denver, Colorado.

point°

Other books you will enjoy, about real kids like you!